THE
IMAGO
STAGE

Karoline Georges

translated by
Rhonda Mullins

COACH HOUSE BOOKS, TORONTO

Coach House Books acknowledges the financial support of the Government of Canada. We are also grateful for generous assistance for our publishing program from the Canada Council for the Arts and the Ontario Arts Council. Coach House Books also acknowledges the support of the Government of Canada through the Canada Book Fund.

LIBRARY AND ARCHIVES CANADA CATALOGUING IN PUBLICATION

Title: The imago stage / Karoline Georges; translated by Rhonda Mullins.
Other titles: De synthèse. English
Names: Georges, Karoline, 1970- author. | Mullins, Rhonda, 1966- translator.
Description: Translation of: De synthèse.
Identifiers: Canadiana (print) 20200157159 | Canadiana (ebook) 20200157167 | ISBN 9781552454022 (softcover) | ISBN 9781770566248 (EPUB) | ISBN 978 1 77056 657 6 (PDF)
Classification: LCC PS8563.E6294 D413 2020 | DDC C843/.6—dc23

For you, Maman

I was born between the publication of Darwin's *The Origin of Species* and the moment *Voyager 1* left the solar system, tracing an arrow of evolution though space-time as it passed.

I took my first breath in a bubble that had been swelling in time lapse since the end of the nineteenth century, an electric maelstrom humming with integrated circuits, machines, and transformed matter, contraptions for every purpose, a blowhole of information, transmission, distention in the shape of a mushroom, like the cloud formation from the Tsar Bomba seconds after it exploded. Like the largest detonation in nuclear history, the entire twentieth century rises up to the moon and then careens off past the Milky Way, its eye on the origins of the universe.

The era in which I was born was like an eye trying to expand its field of vision to encompass the macrocosm and the microcosm, then regurgitating it all through the mouth of the media before which I sat immobilized for much of my existence, cross-legged, in the same position since childhood, hands clapping as I watched cartoons or clasped over my open mouth in silence as the World Trade Center came down.

Yet, of all the disruptive discoveries, electronic technologies, and scientific miracles of the past two centuries, I now use a mask and gloves to map out the horizon of my evolution. Every day for almost a decade, I have found myself in virtual reality, face to face with my pixel twin, trying to embody myself through her.

I had almost done it.

Then my mother started to fall apart.

REALITY

There is no furniture around me, no objects. Only a hundred or so green plants lining the walls of my studio. At the end of the room, a glass wall looks out over the horizon to the west. Thousands of dwelling cubes extend as far as the eye can see.

Between me and the glass wall, there is my mother.

She has her back to me, which suits me just fine.

I never thought I would share a space with her again.

I know we were alone together when I was born. We must have spent time waiting for nothing in particular, doing nothing but discovering each other in complete innocence, at complete ease. I must have observed her from the other side of the bottle of formula she held balanced between our faces. I'm sure she whispered to me all the love a mother has for a newborn. And I must have adored her, with the single-mindedness of first love.

Which may explain why I couldn't abandon her.

At least, not completely.

◆ ◆ ◆

It's snowing today. From where I am standing in the centre of my studio, I see nothing but white expanse outside, filled with noise, like a television screen at the end of the broadcast day a half-century ago.

I never look outside, but my mother's presence forces me to reflexively raise my eyes every so often, as if I can sense a menacing insect nearby.

For a long time during my childhood, when I was planted in front of the television, my mother could approach without my noticing. She would have to repeat my name impatiently three or four times before I would come back to what she called 'reality.'

• • •

Every day, I disinfect my mask and gloves. I say *gloves* out of habit, but they look more like wafer-thin suction cups perched on my fingertips. The mask, which is just as delicate, covers the eye area like glasses, hooked behind the ears, the only difference being that the arms relay sound. The whole set-up weighs three grams. I could use immersion lenses and leave my face bare; I always try out the new models when they hit the market, but I can't stand foreign bodies on my corneas.

Every day, I moisturize my face and my hands. I stretch. I swallow a protein bar and a half-litre of water. I make sure the studio floor is clean. I set down my locomotion mat. I put on the mask and gloves.

And I cross over.

I enter virtual reality, and I reunite with Anouk, my avatar, made of mesh and a patchwork of photography textures in 16ᴋ resolution, who is standing there, before me. Her skin is more lifelike than my own. Her eyes are brighter. Her breath is always even, deep. In resting position, she shifts her centre of gravity from one foot to the other with a subtle movement of her pelvis. She nods, blinks, clasps her hands in front of her stomach. Then, in a slow, graceful gesture, she drops her arms to her sides as she rises up on her toes for a few seconds. And the animation starts over, without fail. Often, as soon as she enters my field of vision, the desire to modify her face or body dictates the avenues of my research.

I have a lot to do today to finish settling my mother into my apartment.

But first I have to reinitialize myself.

I am going to create a minimalist scene, undress Anouk, keep her skin, her eyes, and even the tattoo that has graced her shoulder blades for the past week – a dream catcher with a long feather that reaches down to the swell of her buttocks. I am going to swap out the black mane for a classic chignon, perhaps in silver. Place her in a white environment, with a single source of radiant light. Something simple. To try to restore my calm.

I am going to drop all the emotional trait modifiers for her face down to zero. Purge her of any emotion. Until mine disappears as well.

The past few weeks, I've spent too much time offline, far from the digital ether. I was starting to suffocate.

I have to become an image again. As fast as I can.

I became the image of a woman before I hit puberty. By age thirteen, I had long been dreaming of appearing on glossy paper.

Every week, as fast as a cheetah, I would race up the stairs to my grandparents' apartment to go through the new issues of *Magazine illustré* and *Lundi* that my grandmother would leave around the kitchen, under the crystal chandelier, on an antique table laid with an Italian lace tablecloth. There were no books at my grandparents' home. Only my grandfather's girlie magazines. He wore his love for pin-ups with a blend of pride and mischief and enjoyed showing me his latest flame, prominently on display in his Snap-on calendar hanging in the kitchen beside the buffet, like a constantly changing work of art. The blond ingenues seemed to transform into luscious brunettes, only to lighten the next month into saucy redheads and then go blond again, often platinum. Every month, my grandfather would comment on the new recruit. 'Look at that curve; that's poetry. You'll never see a more perfect small of the back. I mean, the lips on that doll are worth a close-up, but with the delicacy of her areolas completing the picture, we've reached the pinnacle of the art.' My grandmother would burst out laughing, and every time my mother seemed resigned and perhaps a bit ashamed.

My grandmother loved celebrity gossip. She knew nothing about the celebrities, their work, or their talent, only that they appeared in magazines. She didn't watch TV or listen to the radio. She knew nothing about the movies, but she would learn about the stars by reading flash interviews. She also subscribed to *Nous deux*, a strange photo romance magazine that told short, mind-numbingly saccharine stories featuring Italian actresses who could have been models for my grandfather's calendars, they were so similar. My grandfather's infatuation with his pin-ups and my grandmother's fascination with Hollywood stars form the basis of my family's cultural legacy. I learned early on the sacred nature of images of femininity.

The most famous women in the world were all frozen between the pages of magazines. Or sublime on the screen. Or framed for all eternity in museums, something I would learn later on.

I became an image without even knowing it.

It was the mid-eighties, smack in the era of spectacle, the material girl, and fashion as religion. There was a modelling competition at my high school. The grand prize was appearing on a poster for Vrai Coton, a chain of stores that was getting a lot of buzz across the country, a multinational that sold T-shirts, tank tops, and leggings in the neon colours of the day.

I never would have entered a contest like that. I was shy, practically mute, and I spent my days finding ways to avoid attracting ridicule or jealousy – or any notice at all. I had two friends, who were just as quiet, with whom I observed those who knew how to attract attention. We would keep our distance from the anxious crowds, where girls and boys challenged each other in a series of mocking, blustering exchanges, punctuated with flurries of raucous laughter and taunts verging on bullying.

I was invisible. I was uncomfortable when others were around: I didn't know how to act, I couldn't hold my own in a conversation. All I knew was how to watch. Listening without moving, ideally sitting in front of a television screen. But I knew how to fade into the crowd and disappear. And since I hunched a bit to avoid being seen, hardly anyone noticed that I was taller than average, and slimmer, too.

I entered the contest to blend into the crowd, to be like the other girls. Just like every morning, I did what I could to add height to my frizzy mop with a cloud of hairspray, then spritzed my whole body with Impulse body mist. I followed the crowd and found myself standing indifferently under the high school auditorium lights.

Later I learned that my blank facial expression was what won over the jury. I was avoiding everyone's eyes, so it seemed like I was somewhere else, devoid of personality. I had a face that could take on any hue without imposing its own. I had achieved an almost mineral presence by staring motionless at the television screen, slack-jawed and wide-eyed as if hypnotized.

Already I wasn't fully alive. I looked like a static image slipping noiselessly down the catwalk.

◆ ◆ ◆

I wanted to be an image long before I understood that I would have to pick something to do for a living and maybe even study to learn to do it.

Had I been born two hundred years earlier, I would have known from childhood what I would become – my grandmother told me so often enough. I would have learned to work my family's land, keep house, play dolly to practise holding someone smaller than me in my arms. Had I been born a princess, I would have imitated the queen and spun around in circles until exhausted, with a crown on my head, shut away in the impenetrable fortress of my future kingdom.

But I was born in the suburbs, in a bedroom community. I grew up in a bungalow with a full set of appliances. And that's where my mother stayed, sitting at the window in the din of the dishwasher, looking out at the horizon of identical bungalows, smoking a cigarette. She was almost as still as the images of women in my grandmother's magazines, but without the hair, makeup, or designer clothes. She must have moved at some point during the day, when I was at school, or maybe at night. I never knew. But at the end of the afternoon, when I would come home from school, she would be at the window, smoking in silence. And later in the evening, she would go down to the family room in the basement, sink into the sofa in front of the TV with a glass of wine, and sometimes a book, and not move. In the summer, when she was pregnant, she would go out on the front steps for some air. We would walk around the block, her smoking a cigarette and me eating a Mr. Freeze. Then she would miscarry and go back to the living room and her glass of wine.

My mother was pregnant my entire childhood.

Her belly would swell for three or four months, then she would cry for a week. I would hear her whispering to my father that she didn't understand why. And my father would down a large gin.

I could have had nine brothers and sisters. Maybe more.

Instead I had dolls the same size as me, which I would seat in the living room, facing the screen. I thought it would console my mother, that she would find fulfillment in the midst of our little group. But nothing could overcome her sadness, which made her lethargic, her eyes as unmoving as those of my dolls.

Had there been no television in the middle of the living room, creating the impression of constant activity in the house with its endless stream of shows and movies, before which I would sit inert whenever I could, I would have thought I had already reached the realm of the image.

◆ ◆ ◆

I spent most of my life observing images. Or creating them in my head, by reading novels. Before I started kindergarten, I would spend my days bingeing on Japanese cartoons, including *The Adventures of Hutch the Honeybee*. It was the story of Hutch, the bee, and foretold the solitude I would embrace years later, and the terrifying absence of a mother, his own having disappeared somewhere in nature's hostile expanse, while mine was overcome by the burden of death in her belly.

I remember flying with Hutch over marshes teeming with sinister creatures. I dove under water lilies with him. I slept cradled in the middle of a tulip. I danced with butterflies. I faced down monsters with giant pincers, crying and screaming in terror. And I would dry my eyes a few minutes later with American superheroes who could save the world between commercial breaks, or with Bugs Bunny, whose devil-may-care attitude and sense of mischief were matched only by his quiet smugness. Then I liked to lie down on the floor and flip through my father's collection of illustrated books, including a whole row of the bookcase devoted to the history of military atrocities and another on the mafia and the death penalty. Once I learned to read, I would spend hours poring over photos of guillotines, gallows, and other instruments and techniques of torture from the Middle Ages, like torture by strappado and the head crusher, which popped up in Wile E. Coyote's more Machiavellian schemes to capture the Road Runner. I would alternate between the adventures of Asterix the Gaul, Atom Ant, and photos of World War II mass graves.

I discovered the astonishing and the horrifying. Fiction and reality, intertwined.

Yet my anxiety dissipated in the bright glow of the screen. I thought the endless cartoons were thumbing a nose at reality. Death was a mere few-second interlude, and then my idols would be resurrected to continue their pursuits and bring on new fits of laughter.

Through the years, I needed to return, more and more often, to this endless escapade that was unlike everything I understood of the world beyond the image.

◆ ◆ ◆

My first desires were all based in fiction. I would have liked to have stepped through the television screen to hang out with Fanfreluche, the doll who could insert her entire body into literature. I would follow her into the big books she entered to change the course of the stories she was reading.

I already had the urge to be teleported, to slip into a new skin, a new body. To be manifold, to mutate. To have wings or robotic limbs. To discover my supernatural powers or extraterrestrial origins. To travel through time.

By contemplating moving images, by contemplating only those, I lost my taste for reality at an early age.

Before starting kindergarten, I began having science-fiction nightmares in which I would fly on a broomstick like Sally the Witch, but with no control over my movements. For what seemed like hours, I would try to keep my body aloft two or three metres off the ground, or to gain elevation, to move horizontally, avoiding buildings and trees, but I was always sucked back down to the ground, which threatened to swallow me up. I couldn't break free, and I would wake up in a sweat, exhausted by the manoeuvres. The memory of those flights haunts me still. There was no distinction between the memories of my dreams and of daily events. I truly experienced flight, just as I knew how to swim in the sea. In fact, I would fly more often than I would swim.

And I remember it more vividly.

◆ ◆ ◆

As a child, I didn't want to accept the distinction between reality and simulation. What was happening on the screen or in the pages of a novel had more value for me than reality. What I felt while reading or watching TV – fascination, pleasure, curiosity, wonder – was undeniably intense. But I realized early on – perhaps too early on – that I was on the wrong side of the screen.

I spent every summer of my childhood shut away in my bedroom in the basement, curtains drawn, going through two or three novels a day. My memories of that time are contained within the space of a bedroom that was nine square metres and a family room a little more than eleven square metres. That was where my father drank his rum and Cokes as he listened to hits from the sixties, surrounded by a gun collection that he polished once a year and that collected dust the rest of the time as he snored over the incessant explosions of war documentaries. My mother would sit in the kitchen reading Michel Tremblay or Danielle Steel, with her Du Mauriers and her Italian wine. We would each retreat into a cocoon of words, images, or music.

Mid-afternoon, on the days my father worked, I would open the door to my bedroom and walk three metres to sit down in front of the television, my daily source of light. I would go out in the early evening to the small local library to find more worlds to explore. Science-fiction mainly. Or fantasy. The truest form of fiction, the purest, the most powerful. I would go back to my bedroom, open the curtains to a sliver of moon, and dive back into a book.

I tore through stories of hapless good little girls from the Countess of Ségur to the *Le masque fantastique* collection and the Fleuve noir books, where I encountered untold numbers of monstrous creatures. I didn't know anything about literature, not even the word, the meaning of which I learned a few years later in high school French class. I didn't understand the value of the writing I chose at random from the library, but I was viscerally curious. The more strange or fanciful, the more voracious I was. I already liked living through parallel realities, half embodied in several waking dreams at once. I would dive into the gothic world of Dracula in the morning and propel myself into the future once evening came, somewhere beyond the six hundred and twelfth galaxy of an André Caroff novel.

I learned from the start to pay attention to the stories that unfolded on the other side of a window, before which I knelt with the devotion of a nun at an altar. I spent a lot more time studying what fictional characters were doing than observing my parents.

My presence in the world was always turned outward, toward the Other. The being in shimmering colours on the television, the narrator who told of his adventures through an arrangement of words a thousand times richer than the few monosyllables of joual spoken around me at home.

Early on, I understood that real life was happening there, on the screen. Or between the pages of a book. The rest was a chore to be quickly dispensed with so I could spend as much time as possible in unlikely worlds captured by an antenna or printed on paper.

◆ ◆ ◆

Before my mother explained it to me, I thought that what I saw on the screen was actually happening somewhere, live. That television was a sort of webcam before its time.

Afterward, with something like suspicion, I was able to distinguish between fictional characters and the fabulous people of the star system. I saw their mansions in magazines; I started following awards shows and the red carpet, memorizing who was engaged to whom, who had just divorced, and who was a confirmed bachelor. But what first fascinated me wasn't the fame or wealth of the celebrities, but rather the characters they played. These human beings, who could have lived in the suburbs, like me, staring at their televisions, had been chosen to become immortal creatures on the screen. Which meant that the ultimate status you could achieve was to exist there, on the other side of the warm glass on which I often laid my hands to try to touch my idols.

That was my first career choice.

Fictional character, body of light on a screen.

STUPOR

One Monday last fall, around noon, I get a call from my father. I know it's an emergency as soon as he says my name in a shrill rise of inflection. He wants to know whether it's me. My heart starts to race. While he talks, I observe Anouk, frozen in a pose not unlike the *Ecstasy of Saint Teresa*. The light gently grazes the folds of the homespun robe that covers her body and part of her head. I leave the second spotlight I was going to move to bring out the mystical expression on her face. I hear almost nothing. But it doesn't really matter. My father can't get the words out. He is crying. He stammers that my mother is at the emergency room.

I haven't spoken to my father since my last visit to my parents' house, more than two decades ago.

Our last face-to-face meeting was brief. Brutal.

I had just arrived. I was still in the entrance, in my coat and boots, already bothered by the cloud of cigarette smoke that perpetually hung in the house. I had had time to read my father's glassy eyes; he was drunk, before dinner. My mother hadn't yet gotten up from her chair to greet me. Things exploded right away.

A week earlier, a local paper had published a profile of me, talking about my work in Europe, in particular my posing for a group photo, a nude, to raise awareness about animal welfare. Some thirty models were assembled in front of a white background, with soft lighting, no makeup, standing without really posing. The photo was tasteful, but my father was humiliated regardless. What deeply embarrassed him was that his daughter's body was being offered up to his neighbours' eyes. He made no distinction between the pornographic shots in *Hustler* and the stylized ones, with no explicit poses, published in the top fashion magazines. I was naked in his local paper, and the dots hiding my nipples only added insult to injury. My father shouted in anger, glared at me in contempt, then balled up the newspaper, threw it into the kitchen, and said in a deep voice, 'You disgust me.' Then he stomped off to his bedroom. My mother hadn't moved, hadn't said a word; she scratched the back of her right hand with her left. I was so stunned that I didn't know how to respond. I didn't have the strength to defend myself or to say anything at all.

I left.

My father never apologized. Maybe he forgot the attack as soon as it happened; he had had too much to drink. Maybe he always thought I deserved his contempt. My mother never spoke of it either. And for two decades, I opted for silence, too. Silence about the incident. And about my life. And about what I thought about anything at all. I became more superficial than the most commercial of advertising images.

So the day my mother is hospitalized, when I hear my father's voice, even before I grasp the urgency of the situation, I pick up the thread of our relationship exactly where we left off: I am mute, frozen. Incapable of thinking, of reacting. I am afraid of him. Afraid of the slightest word from him.

And yet I listen.

◆ ◆ ◆

After my father's call, it takes me a moment to catch my breath. I release Anouk from her ecstatic pose and take off her robe without finishing the image. She stands there, naked, swaying, carefree, her eyes still closed, her mouth open. Her skin, covered with a marble texture, now looks like that of a stone angel on a tombstone. I am so disoriented that I can't reinitialize her face to restore her bright gaze.

I have often thought I would die like that, in situ, all of my organs stopped cold by a surge of fear. There are words for that sort of thing now: generalized anxiety, panic attack. As a child, I would collapse on the floor with my hands between my thighs, my head at my knees, with a sense of impending doom.

At the time, I knew nothing about climate change, terrorism, the accelerated extinction of species, and the depletion of resources. We weren't worried yet about aliens and the merits or risks of letting our presence in the universe be known. At the time, the scientific community was categorical: UFOs were the hallucinations of crackpot hippies who had dropped too much acid since Woodstock, a decade before. Nor did I know anything about incurable diseases. I would hear about cancer for the first time at the dawn of adolescence, only hinted at, upon the death of my aunt Marianne, whom I didn't know well and whom my father had refused to speak to since she joined the Jehovah's Witnesses. He said it was dangerous to be around her, that she might send us around the bend. I remember hearing my mother cry and say we couldn't let her die like that, without going to her bedside, that the whole religion thing was just a youthful mistake, that there was no God or Jehovah anyway, but that Marianne's suffering was real, that she had already lost all her hair and eyebrows and would soon be dead for good. So I knew then that Jesus's God was a fictional character, the most fearsome of all, which made me want to read all the stories about him.

The threats we heard about at the time were sharks, like the one from the movie *Jaws*, which everyone saw at the drive-in and which gave all of America nightmares, but they were found only in Florida, or so my father said. People talked a lot about drugs, too, particularly heroin, which was killing teen prostitutes in Germany, and which lurked in every alley on the planet, between garbage cans, in unseen rusty syringes on which little girls my age would inevitably step and instantly die before even having lived, according to my grandfather, who had joined Alcoholics Anonymous after having lost his way for more than thirty years.

People were also afraid of the end of the world, being snuffed out by a nuclear explosion. It was the only global threat that penetrated the drywall of our bungalow. But my father didn't believe it. He said we shouldn't *exaggerate*. That no one was crazy enough to *press the button* because everyone knew that everyone else had their own *button to press*. To his way of thinking, the nuclear threat cancelled itself out.

So I had nothing to worry about. In theory.

Except my father.

Who would scream that one day he would kill my mother, or kill us, or hang himself, or tear our heads off, or set the house on fire. Afterward, my mother would explain that he didn't mean anything by it, that it was just the crazy talk of a delayed adolescent, that it was just the way he grew up speaking, that I shouldn't listen to everything he said. That the beer bottles he threw across the living room didn't mean anything either. Nor did the gleeful kicks or mischievous smacks to the back of the head, inflicted without warning whenever the urge overtook him, sometimes at supper when he had had enough of sitting with us. Just drunken hijinks. Nothing serious. Shouldn't make a mountain out of a molehill.

And maybe I could have learned to take my father's melodramatic smacks and insults in stride. You can learn to do anything. You can get used to anything. My mother always said so. But I asked too many questions before opting for silence. And of all the things I found intriguing, death was definitely the greatest mystery. I wanted to understand what my father's constant threat meant, and what happened to the victims of *Jaws* and in all other forms of death, by heroin overdose or nuclear blast. I wanted to understand the death that occurred in TV shows, movies, and even in my favourite Japanese cartoons.

It was Jean, my mother's younger brother, who decided to enlighten me when I was five or six years old. I had seen people on television who appeared to be asleep, eyes closed and mouth open. I had seen them suddenly collapse on the ground. And I didn't understand how the sleep of death could be a punishment worse than a kick. Jean took the time to explain. He asked whether I had ever seen cemeteries. I had seen them, complete with ghosts, on TV. He said that dying meant being shut away in a box, underground, in a cemetery. With the worms and the ants and the spiders, and other insects, too; it all depended on the cemetery. He told me about the cold of winter under the frozen ground. Of the box flooding during downpours. He said, 'Once you're shut away in the box, it's forever.' That was what death was. And everyone died eventually. My uncle was fifteen or sixteen at the time. He had a sense of humour. And a flair for storytelling; he liked television as much as I did. But I thought he was telling me the truth.

The worst threat of all was death. And I would not escape it.

That's when the real nightmares started.

The anxiety became generalized.

I was already immobilized in front of the television screen. From that moment on, I had started turning to stone. I had seen a good witch freeze people around her by wiggling her nose and stopping time, and I immediately noticed that doing nothing, not moving, and, better yet, staring at the second hand on the clock, made time pass much more slowly. If I concentrated, it felt like each second lasted three or four times as long. It also explained the immortality of images that were still. That may have been the secret to not dying: becoming perfectly still, but outside of the box underground.

◆ ◆ ◆

After school, I would have a few moments of respite to tend to my anxiety, before my father came home mid-evening, drunk or in a bad mood and intending to get drunk. While my mother smoked at the window, I would sit in front of the television, not moving.

I was fascinated by many of the characters on the screen. Particularly superheroines and magical creatures. All larger than life. There was Jaime Sommers, the Bionic Woman. She was the first to make me want to replace my body parts with robotic organs. I dreamed of being enhanced, of being able to run so fast that I could slow time around me. I discovered Wonder Woman at around the same time. Every episode, I was dazzled by her beauty. I thought Wonder Woman's near nakedness demonstrated her power. She didn't need pants to protect her from thorns, didn't need a coat in bad weather. Her satiny skin was a living shield.

But of all the television creatures, my favourite was Jeannie, the blond genie in the pink bottle. She, too, wore a sexy costume that showed off her flat stomach. I knew nothing about sex at the time. I didn't realize these characters in bustiers and transparent veils were erotically charged. I was just blinded by their beauty. The pink of Jeannie's costume was all it took to brighten my day. A few notes of the theme song, a few wiggles of the character's cartoon avatar, and I would forget the long hours spent at school learning nothing. The colourful glass of her bottle and its decor of satin and velvet cushions projected me into a dimension of opulence, pure sumptuousness that was a breath of fresh air. Jeannie had that light touch. That way of making everything luminous, without consequence. She loved with an intensity I couldn't fathom. I knew nothing of that sort of love in real life. The happiness other people enjoyed. The desire to be with each other. I just had to shift my eyes from the screen when my mother would walk through the room to feel the bottomless devastation eating away at her. I would get dizzy. Away from television, everything seemed menacing, dark, too heavy. And I had only one desire at the time: to plunge further into the screen.

◆ ◆ ◆

I would also have liked to have known how to pray. I would see the Flying Nun on TV, and her pluckiness and cheerfulness never faltered. And all the other religious characters had a way of being, of looking, of closing their eyes and letting all the muscles in their face go slack. I was impressed by their peace of mind and wisdom.

But I had learned at a young age that religion was the stuff of war, slavery, capitalism, popes hiding under gilded robes paid for by barefoot folk in Africa, and images of Chinese children sold at the elementary school on the Plateau Mont-Royal. That they had taken people for fools through the Middle Ages with that nonsense of buying your way into heaven by sacrificing yourself to enrich the Church and letting it abuse feral children and people with disabilities. At least, that's pretty much what I heard during boozy family suppers, all delivered in an indignant tone.

Yet, among the snippets of catechism I snatched here and there, I was struck by the similarity between literary characters, those who appeared on the screen, and religious figures. In its eternal light, the kingdom of heaven had the texture of a movie screening.

I first found out about Jesus of Nazareth on TV at Easter. Every year, the Saviour's electric blue eyes would bore through the screen as if he were right there, through the same window where I could follow the trials and tribulations of my other idols, fictional creatures whose flesh on the screen seemed as alive as the flesh of the Son of Man. It is worth noting that Jesus was the first poet I ever encountered, in the pages of the illustrated Bible my grandmother gave me. *Love one another. All things are possible for one who believes. I am the bright Morning Star.* Christ's words were as intriguing and fascinating to me as Sherlock Holmes's deductions. My grandmother probably didn't realize that the pretty orange book would end up among the tales, legends, and sagas in my bookcase, where once-sacred texts and wild fantasies existed on the same continuum, all having been read in the same position, lying on my stomach on the bed, feet sweeping the air like wings to keep my attention on the lofty imaginings of writers, taking in everything all at once, their supreme wisdom, their subtle humour, their psychotic delirium.

◆ ◆ ◆

I first heard the word *spirituality* in Paris when I was sixteen, from a makeup artist who was applying an iridescent gloss to my lips. She said all it took was a drop of shine to reveal the soul's sacred light. I didn't understand what she meant, but I raised my eyebrows to suggest agreement.

Two months earlier, I had been shut away in a basement on the South Shore of Montreal. There was no one there to introduce me to spirituality, only people who found the meaning of life on autopilot, a way of being present by default, with enough alcohol in their system to make it through the daily ache of aimlessness.

Perhaps I could have discovered the Sacred through nature. But I had no exposure to that either. The land had been bulldozed to build the housing development where I grew up. There were no trees left in the neighbourhood, only shrubs with a few bare branches that at best looked like fence posts that had stepped out of line. And while a few neighbours planted flowers in the spring, it was generally done haphazardly, with no regard for botany, just purple pansies and sunflowers that slumped under the sun before the summer solstice. Of course, there was the green of the lawns, regular squares scoured clean by pesticides, vaguely reminiscent of the greenery that existed before everything was levelled to create a twenty-first-century landscape, but that looked more like the artificial turf of mini-putt greens.

And there was nothing further afield either. I was born in an area with ten low hills, which were imperceptible in an urban setting. Corn and soy grew in fields that in winter looked like abandoned land. Small stands of pines dotted the landscape of highways, factories, shopping centres, and stores, between which electrical poles sprang up from the concrete, their cables connecting, for better or for worse, the mismatched constructions built during the bleakest architectural period in modern times, between the beginning of the seventies and the end of the eighties, during the aluminum and neon rush, in the midst of the reign of bungalows and warehouses hastily built, with no regard for aesthetics or urban planning, by armies of construction workers half in the bag.

What I first knew of Earth was a residential agglomeration, where hundreds of single-family homes make up a monoculture of brick and aluminum. You can get lost in it, never finding a single convenience store. There are nothing but cookie-cutter houses as far as the eye can see, up to the highway that connects a host of little bedroom communities. And, at the time, it was exactly that, places where the dimensions of a person's bedroom marked the limits of the entire expanse to explore, so you had to learn to transcend. My experience of the world was limited to my endless forays into fiction, an elbow on the pillow to project me into a novel or my face lit by the animated colours of the screen.

And I saw the ocean as well, or at least what you could make of it through the sea of brightly coloured parasols, beach towels, and the oiled bodies of tourists, great hordes of whom gathered during the construction holiday on the beaches of the American East Coast. The real ocean was the ocean of holidaymakers whose screeched conversations masked the sound of the waves. A few times I saw the dividing line between the sky and the sea, and sometimes even the clouds hanging just above, but I was never content with what I saw, maybe because I would immediately be jostled by my father or a group of excited kids or their equally excited parents, who always brought me back to their insufferable presence that I could forget only if I managed to stick my nose in a book.

I was already learning to withdraw from the world and find higher ground.

Truth be told, I had heard the word *spirituality* on TV, but I never asked anyone what it might mean. It sounded like *spirits*, which I knew meant that people would be coming over and that the bar had to be stocked. It meant that animated, heated, often combative conversations would keep me from watching television late into the night.

The only people who came over to our house were my father's co-workers and their wives. And these social obligations would make my mother irritable for a week. The day before, she would open the windows to air out the house. The day after, she would survey the mess, sighing. She would stand in front of the booze stains and the cigarette burns on the sofas with her arms crossed, a hand over her mouth. She would just stand there, exhaling loudly. There was a brief interval when she seemed to enjoy having people over, for the first hour, when the alcohol dulled her discomfort, and her efforts to appear jovial and enthusiastic worked for a while, through a few bursts of laughter. But soon my father would start discussing the union with his guest, and the wives would retreat into the kitchen to get dinner ready. My mother hated being in close quarters with the women she called shrews. Sooner or later they would raise sensitive topics, and my mother would grow cold enough to make them uncomfortable. At the beginning of the eighties, the topic most of the time was divorce or depression. A shrew would start by saying it was good to get away from the daily grind and meet *new people*. The past year hadn't been easy. Her sister or her best friend had *gotten depressed* after a divorce. My mother would empathize with a gesture of the head. She would say, 'Life isn't easy, that's for sure.' She would try to acquiesce, fill the glass of the unfamiliar wife, and down her own. Then, without fail, the discussion would turn to the issue of independence, and the shrew would explain that her sister or her best friend hadn't bothered to protect herself by getting legally married or getting a job, that she had somehow asked for the disaster, that you had to be naive in this day and age to be in a relationship without any form of protection. But nothing was more incendiary than talk of feminism to set my mother off. Evenings when the topic arose later, when she was already long drunk, she wasn't shy about calling feminists addle-brained. She thought the duty to get a job was a new, more malign form of subjugation. She would fume, saying it was always the same story, that after having forced women to obey their husbands, after pushing them to produce a string of babies for the Church, now we were going to bleed them dry to fuel the economy. She said that all women would soon *get depressed* if they insisted on elbowing their way onto the job market. My father and his guest were often galvanized by what she said, finding it hysterical. They would launch into their anecdotes about work: women were never up to the task, they slowed everything down, they weren't meant to work with their hands or their heads, and most of them didn't have an ass to speak of either. Then a fight would break out. My mother would try to clarify what she meant, defend women's intelligence and know-how, and explain that it wasn't a question of aptitude, but yet of another obligation that came with strings, power games, and abuse. They would talk about pay inequity, and my father would shout that it wasn't inequity at all, but rather justice. Everyone was paid according to their skills.

Then he would pound his fist on the table.

And my mother would immediately retreat to the kitchen in silence with a bottle of wine and stand near the sink for the rest of the evening, smoothing her eyebrows with a trembling finger, as she looked out the window.

◆ ◆ ◆

I was already programmed to withdraw and devote myself to spiritual pursuits, or at least worship. Had I been born a century earlier, people would have remarked on my way of melting in front of the screen, my eyes widening on the succession of images, never blinking, or almost never. I realize there was no television at the time, but I would have found something else to stare at. Maybe paintings in church. Or images from the Bible.

I had a visceral fascination with television, but it didn't take much to learn to love still images as well.

The first one that moved me was on an album cover.

It was a picture of Olivia Newton-John, arms crossed, for her album *If You Love Me, Let Me Know*. It was the first record my grandmother gave me, probably chosen because it seemed harmless, with the trees in the background and the sensible-looking young blond woman in a denim shirt and not too much makeup.

I was seven years old.

I fell instantly in love with Olivia.

I felt like her radiant smile was just for me. It was only later that I realized she wasn't smiling at all, at least not in that picture, that it was all in the intensity of her gaze, which kept meeting mine. I don't know why I thought I saw something luminous in her face. Or why I then felt the compulsive need to collect hundreds of photos of her, cut or torn from newspapers and magazines, for close to a decade.

◆ ◆ ◆

My mother never understood why I collected photos of Olivia rather than playing with Barbies or skipping rope on the pavement with the neighbour girls, whom I could have invited for a swim. Nor did she understand my lack of interest in the massive

- 33 -

above-ground pool that filled the yard, which had so much chlorine that I would emerge after three or four minutes of swimming with my eyes burning.

I don't know how I learned to collect. I don't even know whether I was aware of what I was doing. I wanted to spend as much time as possible with Olivia, to be with her where she lived, in the realm of the image. In my favourite pictures, Olivia exuded a lust for life I had never seen before. I was fascinated by her unfamiliar rapture. Everything about her was radiant. Her beauty, her voice, and her energy on the screen. Every one of her pictures revealed a little more of her splendour to me. So I needed to find all the images of Olivia I could to truly experience her.

Olivia was the idol of idols of my childhood, with her sublime smile on album covers and the posters that hung in my room. She was always there, with new movies, new albums, new videos and TV specials. Every week, images of her would appear in *Magazine illustré* or in the few other magazines I would flip through at the convenience store, stealthily ripping the pages I wanted so I could add them on the sly to my collection. I knew that I wasn't allowed to tear pages from magazines, and that I could get caught, but I couldn't just leave without a small piece of her.

I knew nothing at the time about the talent of photographers or the possibilities of image composition. Or, rather, I could tell that our vacation and Christmas snapshots looked nothing like Olivia's album covers. I always looked sad and amorphous; my mother, too. We were blurry. And maybe I thought that one thing explained the other. That our ugliness in the pictures my father took could be compared to Olivia's incredible beauty in her promotional photos, that her broad smiles revealed just how much more alive she was than us, that colours were more vivid somewhere else, and people more joyful, just happy to be. That I had to improve myself so one day I could look like her in our vacation snaps. That I should study her knack for magnificence.

I didn't know what it meant to have a role model. But I knew that I desperately wanted to be like Olivia. And that it had nothing to do with her extraordinary teeth or blue eyes. I didn't notice those details of texture or form. What I wanted was that way of carrying myself with self-confidence, of meeting the world head-on, of becoming radiant to the point that any picture anyone took would reveal that perfect way of being in the world.

I could never have explained it to my mother, but I felt safe when I contemplated my collection of Olivia's silent smiles. Olivia was always radiant, no matter my father's rage or my mother's despair.

◆ ◆ ◆

My worship of Olivia bothered my mother. She may have seen my mystical qualities, which took her back to her girlhood with the Catholic nuns and their insistent veneration of something she felt didn't exist, something that gave them the right to cane her hands and look down on her with scorn, something she had to recite by heart every morning at church without understanding, feeling only boredom and a sort of relentless oppression.

My mother often said that this new veneration of *airheads* on TV may have been worse than religion. At first, that was Olivia's nickname. It was when *Grease* came out. I had spent a week trying to learn the movie's closing dance number, where Sandy gets a complete makeover and turns into a femme fatale, and pandemonium ensues. It was electrifying. I was so excited to see my idol with a new appearance that gave her fresh powers, like Wonder Woman spinning to shed her alter ego as ordinary woman and reveal her true colours. Or like Jeannie, who wore dresses that hid her magic and was in step with the times, but who, with a blink of her eyes, could go back to her timeless, show-stopping look. In this dramatic transformation of image, I saw nothing short of a rebirth. A miraculous apparition, like Jesus during the Transfiguration.

I didn't realize that Sandy's transformation in *Grease* was about the erotic, that the high heels, the lipstick, the cigarette, and the curls were a way of obliterating the image of innocence and virginity and creating a bad-girl persona. All I saw was Olivia, radically changed and yet magnificent, stunning. There was no sensual arousal, not the slightest understanding of sexual games. Just pure love. I must have clapped or cried out during that iconic scene, I don't remember. But I know that my reaction bothered my mother, who was sitting beside me. When Olivia started swaying her hips, so slim in her skin-tight black pants, my mother said, in an exasperated tone, 'That girl is cut with a knife – a body like that isn't natural.' That bothered me. I knew nothing about plastic surgery at the time, and I had the horrifying vision of a butcher's knife sliding along her body, sculpting its lines. My mother wanted me to know that her beauty depended on makeup, that her voice had been altered in a studio by technicians. That there was an entire machine behind her success. That it wasn't as easy as all that. That what I thought of as beauty was an illusion. That it was unreal. She wanted so badly for me to *snap out of it*. To understand that there were more important things in life than shimmying *hussies*. But when I asked her what was important, she sighed and said I was being smart.

I tried to explain that I truly wanted to know what was more important, that that's all I was asking. I would see her hesitate, and sometimes she would respond that family was important. But she hated her own mother, who phoned her every day. I would hear her lie to get off the phone, lie about what was really going on at home. She never talked to her father, or her sister, or her brother. My mother didn't have any friends either; she said it always ended in theatrics because everyone was trying to play their cards right to stab you in the back. I didn't understand what that meant, but the disgusted look on my mother's face put an end to the conversation. The people who lived near us were just as horrible. The neighbour to the left, a schizophrenic, was a monster to be avoided. The neighbour to the right, who, according to my mother, was 'mentally retarded,' was even more of a concern. Down the street, there was the blabbermouth and her neighbour, who was as big as a house and didn't speak to anyone. There were the Anglos, too, just one family in the entire development, whose hygiene was deemed questionable because they didn't take care of their lawn. My mother said it was the culture, that they probably came from Ontario, where no one cared about having weeds in their yard, and that it was worse still Out West.

I needed to know that the grass wasn't greener anywhere else.

◆ ◆ ◆

The announcement of Olivia's pregnancy, in the middle of my teen years, was a cataclysm worse than the nuclear bomb.

I immediately stopped listening to her albums. I rolled up her posters and stuck them behind my shoes, and put my photo collection on the top shelf of my closet. And then I spent an entire year reading horror, going through every one of Stephen King's and Clive Barker's novels. I started dressing all in black. My heart may have been broken. Or perhaps I was grieving.

It took me a while to understand that I was struggling to accept that Olivia was having a child and would become a mother, like mine, and just as sad, too, I was sure of it. It had never actually occurred to me that Olivia could have children. And I had never realized that she was the exact same age as my mother, virtually down to the day. Olivia was one of the fabulous creatures, a character from a fairy tale; I didn't think of her as human. I thought of her as a goddess. Or better still: a fictional character.

Her disconcerting humanity shook me to my core.

The next week, I went to the poster store at the mall, which had heaps of giant images of Hollywood legends, like Rocky, Charlie Chaplin, James Dean, and Marlon Brando, a few portraits of cats, dogs, horses, and flocks of birds taking flight, and images of sunsets on the beach. I needed something to cover my bedroom walls. The lack of images to contemplate when I woke up made me feel like I was shut in my uncle John's underground box.

In the midst of the pile of posters, I was drawn to a face I was familiar with, albeit just a little. I had heard the woman's name and seen two or three of her movies on TV. She was the queen of the Hollywood idols, with a wide, perfect smile, an offhand attitude, and an incandescent beauty. Adding to the fascination, she had died before my birth, and her legend had only grown since. Her name appeared in cursive in all of her photos, like a slogan promoting her. *Marilyn Monroe*. She was the star to end all stars, the archetype for supermodels. Perhaps the female image that had the greatest impact in the history of movies. I left that day with three posters of her and a new conviction: to be adored, idols had to be dead. And to have achieved the status of permanent image.

SPACE-TIME

The day she is hospitalized, after four hours in Emergency, my mother disappears with two nurses into the trauma area. My father can't go in with her. He decides to go home, to sit in the living room and wait.

He thinks of me.

Maybe because I am right there on the wall in front of him.

Me, tiny, with a forced smile, just before puberty. A laminated school photo, yellowed by cigarette smoke.

He calls me. Details his morning: my mother's condition when she woke up, nauseated, her side of the bed wet, then constant vomiting and incomprehensible speech. He tells me how he put a garbage bag between my mother's legs in the car to get to the hospital. He talks about kidneys, poisoning. He is crying. He tells me she is alone. That he might go back. That he doesn't know what to do. I don't know any more than he does. I tell him I will go to the hospital.

I don't say when.

Then I don't move.

• • •

While they undress my inert mother in the hospital, remove her dentures, stick needles in her arms, I do nothing. I just sit on the floor of my studio. After a while, I have Anouk strike a pose similar to mine, right beside me. With the change of pose, the expression on her face becomes neutral, her eyes open, and once again I meet her gaze as it comes to life with the regular blinking of her eyelids. She looks straight on, glances to the left; her interest is drawn to a point above my head. She seems curious, alert. But calm. Unflappable. I stare at her irises, and I let myself be hypnotized by the ocular choreography. I breathe easier.

I know I promised to go to the hospital. I may have lied. That is practically the only thing I am sure of.

The hospital is fifteen minutes from my apartment. I just have to go down to the underground parking level. Pick a self-serve robo-car beside the door. Then be chauffeured by the virtual pilot. I have never used this type of vehicle, but the online presentation promises it is simple and intuitive.

And yet I can't.

I'm paralyzed.

The thought of having to leave my apartment terrifies me.

I stopped going out a long time ago.

I shut myself away during the first terrorist attacks in Montreal. There was talk of a biological weapon after a series of explosions. The manhunt lasted for three days; I stayed shut away for a month. I didn't even go out on the balcony. I started having everything delivered.

At the time, I had gotten into the habit of spending entire days, sometimes close to twenty hours at a time, watching recordings of hit TV shows that lasted around a hundred hours each. It felt like an accelerated mutation; what had previously been a brief moment of cinematographic wonder that lasted barely two hours became an extended sojourn of days on end. I discovered diametrically opposed worlds, from the reign of the kings of the Middle Ages to the end of humankind on a spaceship. I followed the schemes of a biker gang, then was propelled into an amusement park where you couldn't tell the humans from the robots. I got into Russian spies, computer pirates, crystal-meth dealers, the webs of intrigue woven by a group of sinister carnival workers, California physicians, the living dead, paper vendors, the New Jersey mafia, French ghosts. I was delighted. Soon I would immerse myself in virtual reality for just as long. Computer and film technology were converging at the alpha phase of the crossover into a dimension of pure fantasy. And I was one of the first to rush in.

I left my apartment a month later to compare OLED television screens at the underground mall, right below my apartment, in the labyrinth of stores that form the anthill underground. Then came the accident at the Oyster Creek station, with the heavy rain and southerly winds pushing the nuclear waste north. And the subsequent hysteria, pandemonium, and din of contradictory information. I had a stockpile of spring water and protein bars, and an inventory of fibre and dried fruit. I downloaded a dozen TV series and disconnected from the surface of Earth, to better explore it through the imagination of its dominant species on my new screen. Three months later, I took a quick look at the news and saw no mention of the disaster; there had been two other nuclear accidents in Europe since, an attack here at home, five wars were running their course in the Middle East and Asia, and a new reality TV show featuring pornographic games played by a group of Chinese billionaires was setting ratings records.

Recently, I started forcing myself to go outside once a week, on my balcony, to get a bit of sun. Two or three times a year, I take the risk of venturing outside my door, primarily to go to the medical centre on the ground floor, or to try immersion lenses at the underground mall. And I have to prepare myself every time. Self-hypnosis. Breathing exercises to reduce my anxiety. I never go out without my mask. I activate my companion app, which makes a group appear around me, in augmented reality. I usually choose the Super Friends. Batman, Superman, and Wonder Woman start joking around to ease the tension. I don't hang about. I find what I came for and take the elevator back up to my apartment without stopping.

I let Andy, my domestic android, take care of everything else. He already handles the housekeeping and the few groceries I need.

He thinks of everything, even things I don't care about. Like plants, which he has placed around my apartment. And slowly waters. When I watch him do it, he looks at me with his pale eyes and murmurs in a soft voice that they will give me oxygen.

◆ ◆ ◆

I have been living here for close to thirty years; I never wanted to have anyone over, especially not my mother. After my father's last outburst, I would make up all sorts of reasons for keeping my distance. For a long time, I claimed to be living in an ashram in India. Somewhere without electricity or a phone, which explained my silence and my quick call on her birthday. Often it was the only call of the year. In fact, I had been in India, in Pondicherry, for a week, after a private fashion show in Mumbai. I had followed the group of models to the south of India after the show, to learn to meditate. Or at least to try, unsuccessfully. Until I understood that my way of staring at the television was worth all the breathing exercises and mantras in the world, that I already knew how to detach from my thoughts, or better yet, to think or feel nothing at all, or almost nothing, after a few hours plunged in a make-believe world. When I head into another space-time, my hypnotic state shuts down the slightest surface emotions that ripple through me, and they disappear right away.

Even well before my visit to India, I learned to lie to my mother to avoid conflict. Most of the time, I would improvise without thinking, in an impulse that passed for enthusiasm; I would talk fast so she would catch almost nothing. It was nothing like talking, or expressing anything at all, and my mother must have understood the subterfuge. But it generated something that may have resembled sociability. The character I created was entertaining, boisterous, bursting with joy, like the popular hosts of television game shows. I knew how to fill our conversations with a healthy dose of mind-numbing noise. During our annual few minutes of talking, I pretended I still had a relationship with her. I made her believe that our superficial conversations were proof that a bond endured, despite the silence and the distance. I hoped that being out of reach would put an end to our relationship, with no more crisis or conflict. Just a slow dissolution. Our galaxies moving resolutely away from each other with the grace of a celestial ballet.

Four hours after my father's call, I consider giving up on the idea. I am just as paralyzed as my mother on her stretcher. I have to accept that I can't go.

But I hear my father's devastation in a loop. I hear his astonishment. The waves of overwrought sobs. A voice I've never heard. My father mocks, he ridicules, he raises his voice, he loses patience, gets angry, yells in rage. But he never cries.

I think I understand that this is it. There will be no more strained conversations every year, no more lies, no more dissembling. My mother is going to die.

In the early evening, I sit down on the floor near the front door. I have my supplies in my bag. I keep telling myself that I can head out, put one foot in front of the other, get as far as I can, and change my mind whenever I want. I search through the add-ons for my companion app. I find Asterix and Obelix, Lucky Luke and the Daltons, and a dozen X-Men, including Magneto, and I immediately store them in my favourites. I activate the app. I end up with the whole group around me, a joyous cacophony, in Mandarin. I should change the language setting, but the auditory surprise is amusing enough that I manage to pick myself up off the floor. I tell myself again that I can try going out, with no obligation. And come back to create an image, my hypnotic state restored.

Instead I decide to create one immediately.

Which I should have done hours ago.

All it takes is a quick improvisation. I will choose a programmed pose for Anouk; I just received a series entitled *Germination* from an Australian choreographer. Nine variations on the theme of fetus.

One image, I tell myself. Just one.
And then I'll have the energy to venture outside.

When I bought myself a television and a VCR with the money from my first modelling jobs, my mother said I would make myself sick spending so much time not moving.

Later, when I had been modelling for a few years, childhood experts started to report the harm caused by too much exposure to television. It was already too late for me. I had developed an incurable addiction to the screen, to its promise of a better life somewhere on the other side of the image. At the time, people were talking about the link between obesity and long hours spent sedentary in front of the TV, without touching on the fact that this new way of being, still and passive before a window onto a world of endless fiction that flickered in a thousand glimmering colours, laid the groundwork for an entire generation and those that would follow to gradually lose interest in the physical world and embrace the virtual dimension. What mattered, at the time, was what they could see: the beginnings of an epidemic of ballooning bodies, human matter growing misshapen, crashed in front of the screen, which was expanding at the same rate. In my case, not exercising was a way of managing my limited energy stores.

My mother didn't like to cook, and we couldn't afford ready-made meals; my father would mindlessly eat whatever he could get his hands on, with no regard for his diet. On TV I had seen family meals where people talked and laughed around a table covered in dishes brimming with fabulous food in appetizing colours, but I soon understood that was fantasy, and that in the real world, steak was all gristle and bone, and broccoli was so over-cooked that it lost much of its shape on the plate. Veal liver smelled of excrement, and the stench of beef stew was enough to put me off food for two days. Without meaning to, my mother prepared me to choose anorexia as a way of eating.

I had read somewhere, maybe in a sci-fi novel, that evolved beings would get energy from the sun, and that we would all soon lose our teeth, and our stomachs would become long-lasting batteries. A lack of interest in food was a sign that evolution was underway.

And I believed it.

Throughout my childhood, I sat in front of my reflection to watch for my own evolution. I knew that the change would happen quickly, that I would become a woman. Like my mother or, preferably, like my idols. I spent a lot of time searching for the glowing face I saw in magazines to appear, the radiant light that seemed to emanate from the paper smiles. Then I noticed I wasn't the right colour. In the bathroom mirror, dark circles appeared under my eyes and the tip of my nose. I didn't know about lighting. I thought it was just a matter of growing up, that at puberty my face would produce the luminescence that would give it a delicate rosy hue, my lips would become red and shiny, and my eyelashes would grow longer until they created the effect of sequins on my eyelids. I watched carefully for the first signs of beauty, never knowing that the single orb above me in the bathroom, with its yellow light, lit only the top of my head and would never reveal a twinkle in my eye.

But the night I won the modelling competition, after all the excitement around me, after the only rush of compliments I would ever receive during my modelling career, the bathroom mirror offered up the same hideous reflection.

I couldn't see any trace of evolution in my face. It was as if the mechanism were jammed. So I thought my eyes were defective. I thought I needed contacts to better scrutinize myself.

Or, better yet, an external eye.

◆ ◆ ◆

– 48 –

No one in my family had ever won anything, and the news of my victory shook my parents as much as it did me. For a few days, they couldn't stop arguing. The whole neighbourhood had seen the news in the local paper, and congratulations flooded in from all sides. My grandmother cried as if I had just made a success of my life and provided for my old age. I became an image to the applause of my whole school, my entire neighbourhood, and my extended family.

The day after the competition, I wasn't exactly pilloried, but I did feel a barrier of ice forming every time I passed. No one could figure out how a girl no one ever noticed before had just won a beauty contest, and the few supporters who could have become new friends came smack up against my shyness blinders. The prize didn't fix my social anxiety; I had no desire to interact with others, and the sudden spotlight meant that I had to wall myself in, look down at the floor, walk without stopping, hugging the walls and taking cover. I didn't try to hear what people were whispering behind my back or to deal with the hateful looks. My high school became a narrow corridor where I didn't hear anything anymore, neither teasing nor lessons. I was deaf and blind, hermetically sealed.

Ready to strike the pose and stop moving.

◆ ◆ ◆

At my first shoot, the photographer already had another job for me: the makeup artist needed to update her book, and, apparently, I had the face to inspire her. The hairdresser mentioned a fashion show the following week and a girl pulling out at the last minute, a girl who looked so much like me that we could have been twins. In less than an hour, I had three jobs.

Ten of us, from as many high schools, won the same prize. The photo for Vrai Coton was a group shot, with peals of laughter and plenty of wind lifting our hair and our camisoles in the peach-and-pink light of the set. I was the only one who was motionless in the fray, my eyes closed, because I didn't like the chilly air on my corneas, which were already sensitive, probably from staring at the TV without blinking. I may have looked like I was meditating, but the truth was that I had no idea what to do. Camille, who would become my agent, was there, too. At the end of the shoot, she introduced herself and complimented me on how calm and natural I was. With just three or four sentences, she convinced me to join Agence M. Then she went over to my parents, who were waiting in the vestibule, and managed to convince them, too. They clearly didn't understand what being a model meant. Ordinarily, my parents would have smelled a rat or made one up to prove themselves right. My father would have raised his voice to throw Camille off her game and make it clear he was nobody's fool. My mother would have slipped off without really answering, or muttered, *Thanks, it's nice of you, but we'll see.* Maybe they imagined I was going to pose for nice ads, with a tube of toothpaste or a little dog and his dish of food. Or maybe they were still trying to catch up, dumbfounded that their daughter had distinguished herself in anything.

As for me, I was fourteen, and becoming an image seemed as natural and predictable as puberty.

♦ ♦ ♦

I was hardly a blazing star, but in pictures I had a certain affected quality that lent itself to an international career: I seemed distant, emotionless, devoid of presence, like a mannequin in a store window. I didn't act, I didn't pose. The photographer would tell me where to stand, and I would enter the frame like an object on a pedestal. I would raise my arms when the sleeves of what I was wearing required it; I would turn in profile to show off a hairstyle or the lines of a dress. But most of the time I barely moved; I barely breathed. When I had to pose facing the camera and looking at the lens, I would plunge into the same hypnotic state as my long sessions in front of the TV.

My first job with Agence M consisted of wearing jewellery and staring straight ahead. The picture they chose made its way to *Clin d'oeil* magazine and the top of a few revolving earring stands in a chain of stores that sold cheap accessories. I was wearing bright orange lipstick, the makeup artist had drawn a grid of green lines on my eyelids, and red plastic hearts dangled from my ears. My hair was half bleached and teased into a ball above my forehead. I barely recognized my features under the makeup. But the dark circles under my eyes and nose had disappeared. I was cream coloured, from the ends of my hair to my chin, so uniform that my skin looked like melamine. My eyes looked much lighter, too. It wasn't even remotely me. I liked it.

My father raised his eyebrows in boredom and sighed in exasperation when he saw the image, letting me know that makeup and jewellery held no interest for him. My mother reluctantly assured me that it was well done, that I looked professional.

After that, for two years I let them make me up any way they wanted, I wore anything, I posed anywhere. I had no real interest in fashion; I had no particular style. I told myself that it was a matter of maturity, that no doubt I would soon discover a burning desire for a particular hairstyle or the shade of lipstick that would define me. But the opposite happened. I soon stopped caring about my image. There were others who were better at it. I had nothing to say, virtually nothing to do. I worked barely a few hours a month. My mother went with me, without complaint, but without saying anything either. Some mothers drove their daughters to the pool or to dance class; mine waited, smoking half a pack of cigarettes, while people moved softboxes to capture the light of my profile, which would be used to sell hairspray, sunglasses, or bronzer. I posed to evoke spring, with yellow light filtering through my hair, or winter, with a toque and mittens hiding my cheeks. I even demonstrated the pleasures of water, face blank, eyes closed, mouth open, wet hair plastered to my head, thick gloss on my lips, and hundreds of drops of water rolling down my oiled skin.

I accumulated dozens of images in my portfolio, which I would look at afterwards with the same delighted concentration I had for my collection of photos of Olivia.

I was learning to collect myself.

◆ ◆ ◆

The more I became an image, the more challenging became the gap between my daily life in a twentieth-century bungalow and my unrecognizable presence splashed on paper and billboards.

I had no friends anymore. Between jobs, I was alone in the cloud of smoke at home, in front of my own TV, just metres from the TV watched by my father, who was drinking more and more and who picked fights with my mother daily.

I wanted to get away. But I remained petrified in my bedroom. Sometimes I dared to emerge to get some air, going for a walk around the development. I would see children who couldn't yet speak wander away from their sandbox, run away from their mother, and try to make it to the road. I saw their resolve to take off their clothes, rebel, impose their will – something I had never managed to do. As early as age three or four, I sensed that escape would expose me, start a chase I would lose, and that I would end up immobilized again, put back in my place, maybe even deprived of television for having dared run away.

During my parents' endless arguments, I would move with reptilian speed. I knew the signs. My mother's initial sulking, as she avoided my father's eyes when he was telling a story about a grievance or the union, overtime overpaid, or complicated senior-ity. I knew little about what my father did for a living; he would tell neighbours who dared ask that he supervised a bunch of morons protected by iron-clad collective agreements, who didn't realize they all had their heads up their asses. My father came home from work exasperated, with stories of break times abused, tasks refused, and disputes with the personnel department, and my mother would nod or raise her eyebrows between swigs of wine. When she turned her back on him to look at the fridge, arms crossed or one hand slowly rubbing her forehead, I knew I didn't have much time to noiselessly disappear into my bedroom, and I would quietly start creeping that way. The argument would be about my father's repeated absences, his habit of drinking until he was out of his mind, the boredom felt by my mother, who spent her days and evenings waiting for him, the fact that they never did anything together anymore. My father would shout about his responsibilities, his need to relax, the amount of the mortgage, and the price of the furnace that had to be replaced, and if that wasn't enough, he would shout that he had no choice but to do more, that my mother had no sense of reality, that she should sign up for a macramé class if she was so bored. Everything would be inaudible for three or four minutes, because my mother would wail so loudly that his words would be lost in a long cacophony. And all that time, I would be hiding in my closet, picturing myself running far from the house, as fast as I could, until I would lift off and end up in another space-time.

◆ ◆ ◆

Then one day, I did it.

One morning, a few weeks before my sixteenth birthday, my mother miscarried. She drank a bottle of wine, maybe two, in the bathroom, and as soon as my father got home, in the middle of the evening, she announced that she was going to file for divorce. Then she went out to walk around the block, smoking a cigarette.

I was in my bedroom, in the basement. I heard everything: the door slamming, my mother's heels on the pavement, the sound of a glass being slammed down on the counter, the creak of the door to the cupboard where the bottle of gin was kept. Then silence. Absolute silence. My father must have been standing in front of the kitchen counter, a bottle in one hand and a cigarette in the other. After a bit, I heard him moving around above my head, coming down the stairs that led to my room. Walking past my closed door without stopping. Going to the storeroom. Then, with just one sound, I knew it. A long, serrated sound. It was a zipper. He was opening his rifle bag. I heard the cascade of metal bouncing off his workbench as he emptied the box of cartridges to load the weapon.

My father went deer hunting in the fall.

This was June.

I was one metre from my bedroom door, the staircase was next to it, and right above was the door that led to the driveway.

I didn't hear anything else.

I imagined him pointing his gun at me through the thin sheet of plywood that separated us.

And without thinking, with no control over what I was doing, with my heart pounding down to my feet, I ran.

I ran into the street looking for my mother. I walked around the entire development trying to find her, until I came back to my starting point. I stopped three houses from ours. And I saw her go up the driveway, reach the front steps, and go into the house. I felt like I had become a giant heart that was distorting reality around it with its beating. I couldn't see the front door anymore, my heart was pounding so hard everywhere inside me, even in my eyes. I slowly approached the house, but I stayed in the middle of the street. And then I heard it.

A shot.

A bang, a loud one. But apparently too muffled to alert the neighbours, who were watching police shootouts set to rock music on TV.

No one came out on their front steps.

Except my mother. Who was crying.

She lit a cigarette and walked around the block again. I walked with her. She didn't say a word. I didn't ask any questions. Then I followed her into the house. We both heard the snoring of my father, who had already fallen asleep in their bedroom. While she poured herself a large glass of wine, I went down to the basement. I wanted to know. I saw it. A hole in the concrete floor. A crater, the size of my head. My mother came up behind me, with her cigarette and glass of wine. I asked her in a hushed voice whether we should call the police. The question had been burning in my brain since I heard the zipper. My mother looked indignant. I had insulted her. She looked into my eyes and whispered, 'This isn't a police matter. This is just nonsense. We're not going to make a big thing about it.' I didn't answer, but she probably felt the tectonic plates shift inside me. I was terrified, and suddenly I felt betrayed. The gun was lying there, on the ground. A few metres from the bar full of bottles, the contents of which my father would down in the next few days. We both knew how he could lose it and the next day forget what he had done. And yet she continued to deny the danger.

That night, it felt like she had chosen a side.

At the time I didn't know anything about emotional blackmail or the difficulty of reporting domestic violence, or the overwhelming number of bunglers on the police force. Up to that point I had lived in the binary logic of Hollywood, and my father was the villain. There had to be a superhero who would come to destroy him and save us, with a predictable happy ending, all wrapped up in under ninety minutes. But my mother had just gone over to the dark side. She added in an almost calm tone, 'It's easily enough fixed; your father will fix it.'

A week earlier, Agence M had offered me a trip to Paris to be part of its efforts to expand its market. At first I said no, in a surge of generalized anxiety. But at dawn, the day after my father fired that gun, after a sleepless night, I fled. I took the bus and the subway to the agency. I was ready to leave. I knew my mother would try to forget all about the incident, to minimize it, to go back to her routine. I knew, too, that I would never get over the fear of being killed by my father. I would never be able to sleep in peace under his roof. And I was angry with him for it. With her, too. For forcing me to choose.

Between escape and denial.

• • •

In 1986, shortly after the radioactive cloud from Chernobyl had passed over Paris, I was there, in the grey skies of France, trying to spot Europe through the window of the very first airplane I had ever taken.

I didn't know about the nuclear accident before leaving home, but I would hear about it in the hours that followed, as I was settling into my room. Agence M had the use of an apartment in the 11th arrondissement, and the models stayed there when they were working in Paris. The apartment, a large penthouse that belonged to an English aristocrat I never met, had been renovated in the early seventies with seven bedrooms, each with two bunk beds. During shows, some fifteen girls crammed in there. The rest of the time, there was constant turnover, but always with six or seven models in residence. No one was sure how long the woman's hospitality would last. The penthouse had apparently been a known hideout since the beginning of the twentieth century; for decades, cabaret artists from around the world had taken refuge within its walls.

The morning I arrived, two girls were talking about Chernobyl. One was saying that the radiation would soon spread to Paris. The other was saying we would all be contaminated eventually. I had just landed in a country that was home to over fifty nuclear reactors, which could also explode and wipe out all of France, but that threat was apparently less horrifying than the threat of AIDS, which I was also hearing about for the first time, and which, according to my roommates, killed more perniciously and slowly, liquefying the body from within. A kiss was all it took to be infected. Their chatter got louder. Through the open windows I heard the sound of emergency sirens, bursts of chatter and laughter, horns beeping, and something like a background hum. I was unfamiliar with life in the city. And Paris was nothing but noise to my ears.

For a few moments, I felt the anxiety rise in me. Too much information in too little time.

Even before I had unpacked, my withdrawal mechanism kicked in. The eye mask and the earplugs came out. I stopped paying attention to what was happening around me, intending to transform into an actual image, deaf and blind to space-time outside the frame of a photo. I had managed to escape my parents' bungalow. Now nothing could reach me. I pretended to be exhausted and, taking no further interest in what my roommates were saying, I retreated under my sheets with my Walkman to listen to Madonna's new album, *True Blue*, in a loop.

Anyhow, it was out of the question that I would let just anyone kiss me; AIDS was one more brick in the inner wall I was building to protect myself from others. And the idea of being vaporized along with all Europeans by nuclear radiation seemed gentler than being killed by a bullet to the head, between my father's drunken stare and my mother's resigned one.

I arrived in Paris the summer I turned sixteen.

I left eight years later.

◆ ◆ ◆

Most of the models hated the penthouse, which looked like an unfinished renovation site, with matte white walls covered with marks and holes. There was no furniture, no decor, no plants. The kitchen, with its empty cupboards, seemed uninhabited. There was only a kettle, a few cups, tea bags, and a constantly renewed store of meal-replacement bars and powder, in vanilla, chocolate, and cappuccino flavour. They became my dietary staples. A list of rules had been tacked to the wall over the sink. Smoking and animals were prohibited in the penthouse. So were guests. And anyway, the living room was tiny; the space was filled by just a sofa bed and a TV. The bathroom had been renovated like a gym locker room, with several toilets and showers under glaring fluorescent lights. There were fashion magazines everywhere, piled on the floor, scattered in the hallway, most half torn up. The girls used them to vent their resentment in scribbles, with angry words scrawled over faces or clothing lines they hated. The September issue of *Vogue*, the annual fashion bible, had been transformed a few days after I arrived at the penthouse into a graphic album with the graffiti and street art aesthetic of the Kreuzberg area of Berlin. And when defacing them wasn't enough, the girls tore out the pages they were ashamed of, wadded them into a ball, and threw them out one of the large living room windows. There was nothing else in the penthouse. The laundry room was in the basement of the building, in a damp, poorly ventilated room. To use the phone, you had to go to the concierge's apartment on the ground floor. Long-distance calls were limited to five minutes. Noise in general was not tolerated, and there was mandatory quiet time after 11:00 p.m. It was a bit like a detention centre. But with a video store a few doors down, and a library a little past that.

It was perfect.

I was generally alone in my bedroom. The first week, I bought myself a television, a VCR, headphones, and three pillows. I set up the TV at the foot of the bed, and I fashioned a sort of sofa with the pillows. I spent all my time there. Of course, I heard the conversations of the girls passing through who were already imagining having their own loft with drapes and a walk-in closet large enough to store hundreds of pairs of shoes and the top designer creations.

I wanted none of it.

I knew that one day I would have to rent an apartment, that that's what adults did. But the idea of having to fill the space of an entire apartment seemed unthinkable. It was too big, too filled with matter. I preferred to tolerate the strangers with whom I occasionally had to share my room than to go back to my country and learn to stand on my own two feet. Particularly since a cleaning lady came three times a week to clean the bathroom, check the inventory of meal-substitute bars and powder, and change the sheets. Just managing my own laundry seemed insurmountable, even if it was my only responsibility.

Even then, I was unable to take an interest in my immediate surroundings.

And yet I told my mother just the opposite when I called her, at first once a week, and then less and less regularly. I pretended I knew how to do everything, that things were fine, that I was enjoying my time in Europe, that I had made plenty of friends. She would answer me in a flat tone that I was very lucky and that I should make the most of it. When I thought of her, I would picture her sitting in the living room, staring off in the distance, and I would tell myself that I was precisely where she was looking. And sometimes that was all it took to ease my feelings of guilt at having escaped alone what threatened us both.

◆ ◆ ◆

I accepted all the jobs Agence M offered so I could extend my stay as long as possible 5,500 kilometres from my parents. Models were needed far beyond the reaches of fashion. There were images everywhere. And a constant turnover in every sphere of activity. I posed for corporate brochures, pharmaceutical products, and food ads.

I was the foot for a bandage, the smile for a dental office. After three months, demand grew exponentially; if I was available, there was a job. I was glad when they asked me to stay on indefinitely.

Paris was where I truly learned to be still all the time. I didn't want to explore the city. Even the cobblestones on the streets bothered me. I hated walking on them; my legs would immediately start to ache. There were too many textures on walls, not enough space between buildings, too many flourishes of all kinds. It was suffocating. I realized the extent to which my perception of the environment was shaped by a childhood spent in a development of bungalows, with enough space between each one to accommodate three Parisian buildings, and the unbroken expanse of pavement in the driveway, on the roads, and on the highway. I couldn't appreciate the relatively organic structures of old Europe. Everything seemed chaotic, on the verge of collapse. My eye was always searching for straight lines and couldn't find them. I could leave the penthouse in a taxi and wait patiently to arrive at my destination, most of the time a photo studio; I could wait patiently some more during the long hair, makeup, and wardrobe sessions, and then walk a few metres and turn to stone under the lights, for as long as need be.

But I didn't know how to move in space.

Or I barely knew.

A career as a virtually static object was perfect for me. My way of life involved spending as much time as possible being passive, as if already I barely existed beyond the image.

The fashion of heroin-chic models would soon sweep the market, and I would spend hours lying on dirty floors, surrounded by garbage on a set in an alley, or draped on the windshield of a damaged luxury car. I would also regularly be cast to play scarecrows in apocalyptic landscapes or semi-androgynous, semi-alien creatures, caught in arrangements of crumpled aluminum foil, with glints of green or yellow completing the over-the-top, hallucinatory strangeness of the eighties.

I found fulfillment in those divine moments when I would see my face transformed by the makeup and the lights, under advertising slogans in languages I didn't understand but that always seemed like odes to the character I was playing, whom I didn't know, whom I never saw in the mirror.

I just had to spend as much time as possible observing these virtual extensions of myself in the world for them to, perhaps, permanently replace the child trapped in her grim suburb.

I knew my days as a model were numbered; I was aware of the demand my lack of expression generated, and I already knew that my growing fortune would soon allow me to shut myself away in front of a huge television screen and never again worry about the outside world, even less so my family.

IMMORTALITY

Less than a decade had passed between my father firing the gun and the dissolution of our relationship. I went home once or twice a year, most of the time for a quick stop on my way to New York.

My bedroom was just as I had left it, but there was no way I was going to spend even one more night with my parents. I visited them out of duty, always fearing the worst. When I would take my position in the cloud of smoke hanging in the kitchen, I immediately became anxious. I watched them age in time-lapse, constantly coughing, both with the same grey complexion that let the looming illnesses show through. Ten minutes at home and I couldn't stand it anymore. I couldn't stand the smoke, their gloom, the paucity of topics of conversation. Every other time, my father would greet me with a cold nod of the head and go back to sit in front of the television. When he was already drunk and in a good mood, he would sit at the kitchen table and talk for a few minutes. He would talk about snow blowers or lawn mowers, the noise while the neighbour's roof was being redone, another neighbour moving, the furnace that needed replacing, maybe with a heat pump, cracks in the foundation that had to be watched. Windows that constantly needed washing. The price of cigarettes, which you could get cheaper from the reserves. I feigned interest. I faked fits of laughter. I asked trivial questions about the neighbourhood, and I would leave as fast as possible, often within the hour, without having told them anything about my modelling jobs. And every time, I promised myself it would be the last. Nothing was forcing me to go back.

I was disgusted by my hypocrisy. By my pretending I had forgotten he fired that gun.

When the blast was intact, inside of me.

The prospect of seeing my father again after all these years worries me as much as my mother's hospitalization. I imagine him bloated with fat and hate, like the last time we saw each other, like Jabba the Hutt, with the same wild eyes and leaden, threatening gestures. I can still feel the bite of his last insults.

And with each hour that passes, the more I resist. I can't go to the hospital and face him. I keep telling myself that my mother is in Emergency, that she could die at any moment. It's not working. Zero impetus. No motivation. No drive. Nothing.

So I step onto my work mat. I cross over into virtual reality in a panic. I find Anouk, still sitting on the ground. I quickly improvise. I choose the first pose from the file I just received: *Germination_1*.

Anouk immediately curls up into a ball, lying on her right side. Her shoulder looks like it's sticking out of her neck; I adjust it. I get rid of the spotlights and the ambient light; I move the only light source right above her back, I turn it down, put a blue filter on it. I darken the hue until it's almost total night-black. I watch. It's too clean. I add some bruises and wounds to Anouk's body, mud stains to the bottom of her feet. I increase the luminescence of her skin to bring out the details of the blood in the dark. I tuck her head into her intertwined arms. And I'm there. The composition is working. The title comes immediately.

Will We Ever Be Immortals?

I assemble a black box that delimits the circulation area in the virtual reality image. I choose a larger space than normal for the immersion room, ten metres by twenty, to emphasize Anouk's solitude. I make a rendering of the scene; I publish the raw image online, unedited.

And I sit there, in the state that emerges a few moments after I have finished an image. A brief moment of complete silence inside of me. Perhaps even tranquility.

I sit there, between three dimensions.

The dimension of my studio, where my flesh-and-blood body is; the dimension of my virtual studio, where my digital body is holding a pose used to create the image; and the dimension of my online gallery, where five avatars have just appeared. They start circulating around the composition. The favourites counter starts. Twenty-three stars in the first two minutes online. And the comments begin to appear. *With you, sweetie. Hang in there.* I see flashing emoticons offering me a hug. Ten or so of my followers copy and paste the same hug in a string, a choir united in tenderness. Kitties enter the fray with fat, heart-shaped tears rolling down their emoting pouts. I hear the sound of kisses. It calms me. The reactions will accumulate for at least two hours, the time it takes me to go to the hospital and come back. I minimize the favourites counter and the comments feed in the lower left-hand corner of my mask, I activate my companion posse, and I manage to open the door to my apartment and walk down the empty corridor, with the X-Men leading the charge and the Daltons taking up the rear. In the elevator down, Obelix describes the boar he had the night before, the best he has ever had. Five minutes later, I get in a self-serve robo-car for the first time. Batman stands on the roof of the car, fists on his hips, unflappable. It's a small cabin with two seats, the ceiling is the right height, the seat is comfortable. The departure is smooth. In the lower right-hand corner of my mask, I stare at the blue dot that shows my location on the map. I know where I am. I know where I'm going. I can do this. I repeat that to myself over and over. But it isn't enough to calm my anxiety. I have to deal with a knot in my throat and waves of dizziness. The robo-car drops me at the entrance to the hospital and goes to park in the lot, awaiting my next command. And I stand there, my heart in my mouth. I try to tell myself that the ordeal will be over soon.

I picture what I have to do, imagine myself moving fluidly, quickly, with confidence. Walking toward the emergency room doors, spotting the crowd in the distance. Looking back down at the ground, just ahead of the movement of my feet propelling me forward, listening to the inane chatter of Averell Dalton, who is as hungry as Obelix. I just need to find the information desk out of the corner of my eye, approach it without stopping, accompanied by my posse.

I just have to see the space I am crossing like scenes from a video, to turn into a camera, an abstract eye, to perceive nothing but the mobile presence of people, with a decor of moving colours and shapes. I have to convince myself that they aren't really there, that they are just images in a virtual environment. I imagine that I am still on my work mat, in my studio.

I imagine that this entire scene at the hospital is a simulation, with the definition set a little too high.

always knew how to keep my distance, play the ghost in front of the screen, the blurry shadow in the crowd at school. When I was modelling, I would disappear between shoots or stand silently in the commotion of the wings of a fashion show. I later learned that it was one of my greatest assets. Designers love low-maintenance models like me, who take up the least amount of space possible, who know how to be still, mute, with no moods or emotional outbursts during wardrobe, makeup, and hair. They will tolerate the whims of a select few stars, but it was preferable that the mass of working models, of which I was one, express nothing at all, no admiration, no fear, no aversion or appreciation for a hairstyle or accessory. To endure in the land of the image, you had to embrace your stillness. The slightest abuse could accelerate the sagging of the skin. Bursts of laughter transformed fine lines into permanent wrinkles; the consumption of alcohol altered all functions, but particularly the sense of balance, indispensible on the runway. To be selected repeatedly and achieve immortality through the image, you needed to find a way to slow your vital functions, to opt for a sort of generalized immobilization, in silence, while awaiting the next click of the shutter.

And my way of being ever absent, avoiding eyes and conversation, was seen as a sign of respect and professionalism. I didn't ask questions, and I answered those asked of me with brief gestures of the head and monosyllables. I avoided sudden movements; I was docile and passive, flexible and malleable. I intuitively understood how to play by the rules. I saw taller, thinner models with more feline walks be dismissed after two or three shows for having been too exuberant, too agitated, too grateful to be there, for having dissolved into tears at finding themselves face to face with a legend of fashion or photography.

Whereas I didn't have to pretend to be detached; I didn't know a third of the top designers I walked the runway for. I listened to instructions and I did what I was told, then I would immediately leave to avoid the socializing, the benders, the private parties, orgies, after-hours bars, with the ready excuse that I needed to rest for the next job. But the truth was that I preferred to observe the display of youth and wealth, sexual deviance, and other manifestations of contemporary vice through the cinematic eye, tucked under the covers, expressionless under a clay mask.

◆ ◆ ◆

At the Paris penthouse, I knew how to smile and nod to greet girls I would run into in the bathroom, but I would walk around with my Walkman on, eyes glued to the floor to avoid further contact.

I would spend time with Camille, who guided me through the labyrinth of photo sessions, runway shows, and other jobs. She was my only human signpost.

Camille had just finished her master's degree in art history and had left university, but the desire to go on to a doctorate was gnawing at her. She would pile her books on the kitchen counter in the penthouse, and I would often open one at random to read a few lines. The words were complicated, even unreadable. *Mannerism, neoclassicism, surrealism.* I tried to understand what the whole strange lexicon could mean.

But I was stunned by the works I discovered.

While I was becoming a model myself, the art history textbooks showed images of women from every continent, the same age as me, who had struck a pose and travelled through the centuries to meet my gaze. And I was stunned by the intensity of their presence.

Their way of telling me the story of humanity and its imagination. And, above all, its quest for an ideal.

I spent hours studying the perfect faces, frozen in paintings or moulded in bronze, which seemed to belong to another realm of the living.

'The first faces of the sublime,' Camille murmured, before diving back into her learned reading, where she was trying to understand the evolution of the representation of the female absolute.

◆ ◆ ◆

Camille was about fifteen years older than me. At first glance, she looked washed out. Her hair was neither brown nor blond. She had average, regular facial features: grey eyes, or maybe blue-green. She was neither skinny nor fleshy. She was short. Even very short, in our land of giants. But she had a way of carrying herself, a pace, and gestures that commanded immediate respect. Everything about her was new for me. Her thoughts about the world, art, and beauty were fresh perspectives. When I was with her, my love of the image was no longer deviant, confirmation of a superficial mind, but, on the contrary, indication of a superior quest, a desire for elevation, intelligence, harmony, transcendence.

But what I liked most about her, perhaps, was the way she would talk without asking me questions. She would barely look at me. She had a lot to say, and I had everything to learn. I had nothing to offer in return other than an attentive ear. She understood that I knew how to think, but that I had no desire to express what inspired me. I soon realized that I had nothing to fear from her, that we could establish a perfectly one-way relationship, and I got into the habit of sitting beside her, waiting until she would speak, as if she were a living, breathing television station.

When we met, she had just broken up with her boyfriend, who could no longer deal with her lifestyle, which was increasingly restrictive. I never would have asked the question, but other models wanted to know, because everyone was interested in Camille. It took only a minute or two in the penthouse living room for a conversation led by Camille to generate a discussion between strangers passing through who, otherwise, would have kept to themselves under their Walkman headphones. I knew from my first week in Paris that Camille was part of the straight-edge movement, a subculture of hardcore punk. I had always associated punks with green-mohawked rebels wearing leather dog collars, studs, and ten-eye Doc Martens, but Camille embodied a reactionary, more intellectual strain, with her rejection of baby-boomer values, a rebellion she expressed mainly through abstinence from alcohol, drugs, and even medication. Since I already hated alcohol and cigarettes, which I associated with my father's madness, and I had feared all the rest since I read *Christiane F.: Autobiography of a Girl of the Streets and Heroin Addict*, I immediately agreed with this philosophy. I would adopt it from then on.

◆ ◆ ◆

Four months after my arrival in France, Camille invited me to the Louvre. It was the first time I had ever been to a museum. She initiated me in art history, one work at a time, and in the quest to represent the world, a timeless form of memory, rooted in matter. I didn't say a word during the entire visit, but the emotion that left me speechless was apparently glorious – at least, that was what Camille told me a few years later.

Standing before Géricault's *The Raft of the Medusa*, the piece at the Louvre that looms largest in my memory, I felt something like a heavy blow, followed by shivers. I had seen hundreds of horror movies, with thousands of tattered zombies, blood-smeared cadavers, and slimy, diabolical, misshapen extraterrestrials. But this group of shipwreck victims crammed alongside human remains was the most powerful thing I had ever seen.

I thought of my family, on the other side of the ocean.

I thought of all of my ancestors on the raft, even though I knew almost nothing of my origins. I had had images in my head since childhood, most of them fuzzy. On my mother's side, some had fled the poverty of Northern Italy; on my father's side, they had come from Ireland or Scotland, no one was sure. What I knew was that they had all crossed the Atlantic with pretty much just the shirts on their backs, no fortune or promise, ready to start over. To build everything from the ground up, in a sea of mud and snow. With almost nothing to eat. Not knowing how to pray either. And I have often wondered if there wasn't a bit of my ancestors' despair still running through my parents' veins. Something that fuelled my father's constant drunkenness, when, after centuries of austerity, he had managed, with no education and by the age of thirty, to secure his own kingdom. With his nine-thousand-square-foot lot and his single-family home. His station wagon and his weekends sipping cocktails by his above-ground pool. In this great escape, setting out to conquer a new world, freeing themselves from the clutches of religion, my parents should have achieved a state of grace, laughing hysterically, arms outstretched to the sky, health insurance and social insurance cards in hand, and all the credit they needed to take their inebriation to the cruise ships of the Caribbean or poolside at one of the thousand Resort Inns built just for them in tropical paradises. But it didn't matter that they were born in North America, far from the concentration camps of Germany, far from the first atomic bombs dropped on Japan, in a land overflowing with natural riches, space, and opportunity. Something rotten dictated how they made their way through the world, as if they were being crushed under the weight of a generalized disenchantment that even the best comedies on television could not relieve.

I stayed there for a long time, thinking about my family while contemplating *The Raft of the Medusa*. About our history, told in a single image. This image. This group drifting, decomposing. But still advancing. With no destination. I felt tears well up in my eyes. I had just had my first aesthetic shock. Or a poetic one. Or philosophical, perhaps.

I had come from so far away.

◆ ◆ ◆

When I lived in Paris, I would often accompany Camille to the museums and art galleries. And when I travelled, in Asia or the Americas, I would continue to explore.

With modelling, I travelled around the world, or pretty much, and I went in search of the Eternals, as Camille called them, those sublime images of women who sat enthroned at the pinnacle of art history.

And I got to know virtually all of them.

Camille and I developed a childish game: finding a qualifier to describe each of the Eternals after less than a minute of observation. It was the only time I would say anything, and the exercise entertained me.

I contemplated the delicate Venus by Botticelli and the more androgynous de Milo version; Delacroix's stunning *Liberty Leading the People*; the extraordinary *Grande Odalisque* by Ingres; the adequate *Olympia* by Manet; the incandescent *Woman with Shell* by Bouguereau; the sublime *Venus Verticordia* by Rossetti. And I so wanted to resemble the *Girl with a Pearl Earring* by Vermeer. To tap into her timeless grace, her way of being both radiant and elusive.

I was fascinated by their presence. Nothing of their flesh endures on the canvas. Nothing of their hopes. Their personality. Nothing of the anxieties that gripped them. Their entire family lineage no doubt petered out long ago, the story of their existence disintegrated. Often nothing is known of their identity. And yet they are there. Radiant. Ubiquitous. Reproduced in photos. Projected in the classrooms of the most prestigious universities in the world. They transcend both the canvas and the photographic frame that transport them around the world.

They are neither living nor dead, Camille would often tell me; they exist outside space-time, in the dimension of the Ideal.

All it took was a single visit to a single museum for me to realize that images didn't suddenly emerge with the movie screen or magazines. They have been there for centuries, their imposing presence felt as we raise our eyes and then bow our heads before something that exceeds our grasp. I already knew about the folly of collectors, who paid tens of millions of dollars to own a sliver of this window onto the sublime.

And often, sitting on benches in museums, I would try to hold my breath and stop moving. Without knowing it, I was practising a form of meditation, and every time I started to breathe again, I would feel incredible calm. At the time, I didn't associate my serenity with these exercises, but rather with my ongoing attempt to transform myself into a still image, even outside of photo shoots, the type of image that increasingly appeared to me to be the place where perfection was found.

A culmination, unalterable.

Where nothing changes.

The end state.

◆ ◆ ◆

Camille liked studying the etymology of words. She kept saying it was the basis of all research, the starting point for understanding. When she explained the meaning of the word *image*, at first I thought she was mocking me for my lack of culture. I had always worshipped the image as if it were a window onto a better life, a life more alive.

'Not at all. It comes from the Latin *imago*, which means *death mask*.'

Then she introduced me to strange relics made of wax or plaster, masks created from actual corpses that preserved a trace of the deceased before they rotted and disappeared.

A little later, she pointed to another definition in the dictionary: '*imago, the final stage of development of an individual, among arthropods and amphibians*.' Then she showed me mortuary photographs from the nineteenth century that featured the living and the dead arranged so you couldn't always tell who was who.

I was amazed. I was starting to understand. The image is a form of the absolute, of a whole truth that substitutes for movements of the body, matter, time. Photography can invent the traces it preserves.

It creates a bridge between reality and fiction.

Between life and death.

• • •

In Paris, I learned how to look at myself. Naked. Alone. In a portable mirror. It was something new to me. Often harrowing. But it obsessed me.

I spent so much time hiding under increasingly voluminous costumes, in outlandish shapes, that I always felt like I was transforming into a disembodied figure in the style of the Cubists. In the mid-eighties, the art of being a model involved embracing a form of aesthetic schizophrenia. During fashion weeks, radical images of the post-industrial world flowed with an exuberance never before seen. I went from the monochromatic world of Comme des Garçons – where I was to arch my back under the complicated post-atomic rags of Hiroshima chic – to the sumptuous arrogance of the extravagant gilding of Thierry Mugler, which required playing a bitch in the superficial manner of *Dynasty*, then to the pop intensity from the imagination of Jean Paul Gaultier, which I never managed to pull off, except with movements of the head and arms to signal deliberate madness. I was a hundred fictional characters in any given week, but most often I was a figure all out of proportion, a humanoid hanger wearing creations of titanic dimensions, with pads that tripled the width of my shoulders and hairstyles that doubled the height of my head. The makeup distorted my features: my nose curved to create an aquiline profile, my eyelids grew heavy to look almost Asian, my mouth seemed to collapse onto my chin.

So at night, alone in my bedroom after a shower, I would observe myself. Just me. My reflection. Which seemed strange to me. I didn't know what I was looking for, but I was driven by an irrepressible curiosity about my own anatomy.

I also started observing photographers and their assistants, sometimes trying to talk to them before photo shoots; suddenly, I was asking questions. About the equipment, the tools. I wanted to understand depth of field, shutter speed, light calculations. I took private courses to learn the rudiments of developing and enlarging.

I was learning what I needed to know to turn myself into an image. On my own.

◆ ◆ ◆

I started with a Polaroid.

Because I could photograph myself alone in my room and immediately see the result. The pressing need to make myself into an image demanded efficiency. Yet I only barely understood the importance of the lens when shooting. And I thought that the light from the flash always worked, illuminating evenly, like heat perfectly distributed in a microwave. I was wrong. The flash flattened my face. And the camera lens distorted it as soon as I tried to do a close-up. Then there was the automatic release that allowed me to pose at a reasonable distance. But the result was similar to the pictures my father would take. Blurry and sad, with no definition, and greenish hues.

I needed proper tools. So I bought myself a Pentax K1000, the camera photography students were using at the time, with a tripod, a lighting kit, and – an essential gadget for my project – a remote switch.

My interest in photography was specific: I wanted to make self-portraits. And nothing else. Had I been born twenty years later, I would have taken to the selfie like religion, but at the end of the eighties, taking pictures of yourself seemed contrary to nature. The preparation was long and risky, the result uncertain.

For two years, I tried to capture my image. I would keep my makeup on at the end of the day of a photo shoot, I would go straight back to the penthouse, I would retouch my nose and forehead a little with mattifying powder. I would settle in on my pillows, and I would slowly move my face in the beam of light, regularly activating the shutter release.

When I started taking my own picture, I had already posed for about a hundred photographers who had made me look like a hundred different girls. And while I liked the illusion of always being new and unrecognizable, it was inevitably more of a surprise in black and white. Camille said it was a matter of taste, that my austere, minimalist character was best expressed in monochrome. But I had the impression that the black-and-white image was even more true, that it didn't try to create the illusion of reality, which I wanted no part of.

Every week, I would take some 360 self-portraits. About ten rolls of film. I had access to a darkroom in the neighbourhood. It was poorly ventilated, dirty, and the hourly rate was exorbitant, but it had the equipment I needed for my research. I would run into photographers I worked with, but most of the time they didn't recognize me. Or perhaps they were too absorbed to take an interest in what was going on around them. Most smoked Jamaican hash all day, with a few lines of coke to perk them up at the beginning of a shoot. So I was left in peace.

I would shut myself away in the darkroom one day a week. I would see my face emerge in the developer, always with too much light or a poorly balanced play of shadows, movement, and blurring that were at times poetic but never flattering. I worked blindly, trying to outsmart the eye of the lens to force it to show what I wanted, without knowing what I was looking for. After every session in the darkroom, I would set up the same lights, with what I didn't like in mind. I would close the barn doors a little more, I would move the light back or forward, I would raise the tripod two or three centimetres, move it one centimetre to the side; I would close the shutter a notch; I would make sure I relaxed my jaw and pinched my nostrils. I would wait until I felt a hypnotic state come over me. That's when I knew my gaze would be blank, and I would activate the shutter. I would go back to the darkroom with my load of film, my box of paper, and my bottles of chemicals. I would shut myself in the tiny closet and wind a first roll of film onto the spiral, then a second. I would prepare the developing solutions, set the timer, and shake the developing tray a little faster or slower to try to find the perfect technique. I would move on to the fixer, rinsing. I would unwind the film to see what enlargement would confirm: that my image was still amorphous.

The images other photographers made were clear: I became someone else, through the layer of makeup and the reflection of the light on the pigment of the colours. I was the piece of clothing or the product, I was the retouched profile, I was a silhouette on a set under a brand name. In front of my own lens, I had a familiar face, but with no distinct features, like the absence of presence.

I was virtually imperceptible.

I didn't know how to find the light, or the right angle, or the right pose. After two years of exposing my face a few centimetres from my 85 mm camera, I gave up. I didn't know how to appear.

I was resigned to posing for strangers who made me into a stranger, too. Infinitely different from one image to the next. Endlessly unrecognizable.

◆ ◆ ◆

The eight years I spent in Paris felt like a reprieve, in a zone without time.

I no longer felt the terror provoked by the hate-filled looks from my father or my mother's distress. No matter the chaos on the set or the mayhem backstage at fashion shows, I felt no real threat. Everything seemed predictable, appropriate. Easy. The gentle, swift hands on my face, the instructions to close my eyes, open my mouth, lift my chin a little more, and not move. Effortless. The speed blowouts, the bobby pins slid along my scalp to hold strands of hair stiff from layers of gel, mousse, and hairspray. I barely felt the tugs, which were few and soon forgotten. Sometimes there were minor assaults. Large clips on the back to adjust the waist of clothing for photo shoots, which restricted my breathing; the blinding spotlights; the rhythmic click and the panting bad breath of most of the photographers who would dart around me like angry wasps. I was repeatedly insulted by capricious clients who judged my appearance as if I were one of the pieces of clothing I was to wear. And I heard it all: I was too short or too tall, hideous or too cute, shamefully sensual or not bony enough. They would observe me, commanding me to turn with a slap on the shoulder like a top meant to spin on its axis, rotating perfectly uniformly. I saw all the frowns: the annoyed frowns of makeup artists who found my skin too grey or too dry, my mouth too ill-defined, and my eye colour too wishy-washy, in need of coloured contacts, which I couldn't tolerate for more than a few minutes. I saw the irritated frowns of hairdressers who couldn't find the body in my hair, which was as flat as my expression. I saw the dumbfounded frowns of celebrity portrait photographers, used to the dance of seduction, from whom I would hide out of habit, and who didn't know how to make the most of my lack of presence.

But I had seen and heard much worse at home. My father had been watching me with disdain since my birth, adding a dash of hatred, an exasperated sigh, and a volley of insults, if he wasn't drunk enough to pass out as soon as he got home from work.

In my line of work, there was a certain sophistication in the art of the insult, something more refined. I never felt violent hatred from clients or photographers. The ones who didn't want to work with me avoided me rather than trying to annihilate me with a crazed look like my father. His insults, delivered in a booze-soaked voice, had prepared me for worse. They could call me any name they liked; the French and the Italians were masters of the art of the drive-by insult, launched with passion and quickly forgotten. They could make me wait, never considering my needs, or pull my hair and make me wear degrading things. I was numb to mistreatment. Or, rather, I no longer had the energy to muster any emotion. My childhood state of generalized anxiety had given way to a sort of indifference. I observed, nothing more. I just had to turn to stone in front of the screen of the world, and all the shows would follow, one after the other, in a continuous stream of noise and chaos, fits of laughter and theatrics; there were magnificent people and monsters, all interchangeable, and I would be their faithful audience, always.

◆ ◆ ◆

In 1994, the calls started to drop off.

In the spring, the owner of the penthouse died, and her heirs politely and promptly evicted us. In the wake of this, Agence M announced that they were restructuring; a dozen jobs were cancelled in one week, and I found myself with nothing ahead of me. I returned to North America feeling like I had been thrown out in the street.

Yet, by virtue of eating almost nothing, never going out, living free at the penthouse, and taking all jobs I was offered – from nail polish ads to local runway shows by designers who faded as quickly as they emerged, from travel catalogues to television ads for alcohol and restaurants – sometimes doing three photo shoots a day for weeklies and monthlies, I had saved enough money to withdraw from the world for more than a century. Provided I continued to live fairly modestly.

But I was still terrified by the idea of having to find a place to live and to take care of it.

That was my first reaction when I heard we were being evicted: where will I go? There was no way I was going back to my parents' house. And there was nothing keeping me in Paris. Camille seemed as bereft as me. I didn't yet know she had just resigned and that she would soon be going back to university to work on her doctorate, to return to her coterie of intellectuals. I didn't yet know that she would promise to come see me and that I would wait, for years. She didn't tell me about her plans that day. But she offered me guidance, one more time. She had heard about a high-rise that had just been built in downtown Montreal, connected to the underground city. Two other models had moved into it. I didn't look around to find anything better. The mere prospect of having to pick somewhere filled me with anxiety. Camille had pointed the direction; I followed through. Less than a week later, I visited my first apartment, on the twenty-seventh floor of Place Centre. A four-room apartment as white and empty as the penthouse in Paris.

And it would stay that way. I knew when I approached the glass wall where my mother is now that it was right for me. I couldn't hear the sounds of the city. The horizon seemed hazy, the sky vast, movement on the ground fuzzy. There was only the immobile verticality of the buildings at my height. Utter stillness.

I was tired.

SUBSTITUTION

After hours of dread, I am here. In front of the door of the trauma area at the hospital.

My father is here, too. Sitting alone, in the middle of a row of plastic chairs.

My companion posse has disappeared. Joe Dalton was bragging about being taller than Asterix – who was laughing and rolling on the floor – when my mask went back to being a simple transparent surface. I can't hear anything else; I am not connected anymore. I discover later that the hospital is a wave-free zone.

I suddenly feel naked. Exposed.

Yet the terror I thought I would feel when face to face with my father doesn't come. Nor the anger. There is no dramatic turning of the tables either. No emotional climax like in the movies, with a leap of the heart, redemption, and unconditional love that conquers all and enables the reunion and reconciliation of the father with his progeny. There wasn't even music in the hallway.

Only strangers, circulating around my father, not paying him any attention.

He has aged.

He was massive, imposing. Now he is a frail man, half bald. His hands, disfigured by deep wrinkles, move frenetically from his ears to the top of his head, making a few silver hairs stand on end, reflecting the fluorescent lights. I approach him hesitantly, already wanting to flee; I stop a metre away from him, unable to advance any further. And I stand there, without announcing my presence. Yet this man is not the same one who terrified me. There is nothing left of the monster from my childhood. After a moment, he notices me, gets up, staggering, his eyes unfocused, looking elsewhere. He doesn't greet me, doesn't try to bridge the distance between us. He avoids my eyes. In the weeks that will follow, he will never look at me.

He murmurs, 'Your mother will be happy to see you.'

That's it.

He moves away, without a word.

The situation is so strange that I stand there, trembling, a knot in my stomach.

Afterward, orderlies, androids mostly, pass each other in the corridor, disappear, are replaced by others, all moving with the same quick step. I stop one. I ask to see my mother. He guides me through a maze of machines, plastic sensors, and electrical wires under harsh lights, to a stretcher around which two nurses in face masks are bustling.

When I see the body lying under the greenish fluorescent light, I understand my father's horror.

I can see the oval of a face without colour, two nostrils, a thin line where a mouth should be. I notice the web of wrinkles that runs between the mass of grey hair and the neck of the hospital gown, a fabric of folds, bumps, and divots. I can make out the catheter that runs up between her legs and the catheters in both arms.

But I don't see my mother.

◆ ◆ ◆

I approach, bend over her face. I observe everything that the fluorescent light reveals. I search for a detail I recognize.

Nothing.

With her eyes closed and no dentures, the paper hat covering part of her hair and the mint-green gown are like a form of extreme camouflage.

If she would just open an eye. Just one. I would immediately recognize my mother's iris. Coffee colour, with black lace around the pupil.

If she would just extricate one of her hands from the sheet tucked firmly around her, I would recognize her fingertips, particularly the index and middle finger that held cigarettes perfectly level between her lips all day long during my childhood. But there isn't the slightest stench of tobacco emanating from her.

So I leave.

◆ ◆ ◆

That night I have a lunar portrait in mind. In black and white. A profile with low-key lighting, the face emerging from the dark. Or plunging into it. Working with the light source to draw the fine white line on Anouk's face, I struggle with the proportion of features. The nose seems too pointy, the nostrils too flared. The lips jut out under the nose, puffy as though they have been injected with collagen.

For years, I have used images to study precise, subtle body language, a state of being manifested through the play of lines of facial features, expressed in the height of the eyebrows, their shape, the ascending or descending curve of the mouth, how open it is, where the eyes are looking in space. In that moment, my avatar's face looks like a crude, cartoonish pastiche.

So, for hours, I undo Anouk's profile and rebuild it with new settings. I get rid of the nose, then the lips, then the cheekbones. I bring out the chin; I lengthen the line of the forehead. Until my crescent moon appears.

And then I see it.

The decomposition.

The persistence of the emaciated face, which I spent too long observing under the raw lighting at the hospital, emerges like a watermark on my creation space. My imagination is branded, like a plasma screen left too long on a channel that displays its logo, creating a permanent artifact.

What I see is my mother's face.

It's her.

In observing Anouk's metamorphosis, I suddenly feel my mother's presence through my entire body. And I notice a smell. On my fingers. The reek of cigarettes. I must have put my hands on the sheet; maybe I touched my mother's hair when I was standing beside her. I don't know. But I feel like I am emerging from a long stupor and seeing everything on a delay.

I am so afraid that I erase all the changes to my avatar.

And, for a few minutes, I remain, in a grey zone. Neither immersed in the virtual continent nor in my studio.

I am somewhere near my mother's stretcher.

I sense I am trembling. But I can't move. I am still standing on my work mat. Erect, petrified. Barely breathing. And I cry, silently.

The tears roll down my face, between the mask and my skin.

♦ ♦ ♦

Then it comes.

The urgent need to dive back into the digital ether.

To cross over, beyond matter, as far as I can go.

So I connect to the kawaii circuit.

Of all the virtual worlds I spend time in, it's the most colourful. Thousands of avatars gather there day and night, creating a massive city of festive displays, everyone receiving surprise packs, filled with hearts, affectionate thoughts, and funny costumes to wear to join in on the show.

That night, I receive a dragonfly skin with a shimmering comet's tail; in the large anteroom, hundreds of dragonflies are flitting around each other. Some of them emit short melodies, others buzz. The animation that comes with my skin generates a rhythmic phrase with high-pitched percussion. Every newcomer adds to the performance, and everyone is greeted with wide smiles. The stats graphic shows that a dozen avatars from China have just joined us, then two from Brazil, then three others from Norway. And on it goes: every minute, new dragonflies from around the world join the gathering. Friend requests appear by the dozens in a pink square with royal gilding. I accept them all, though I will never communicate with any of my new contacts. It's the thought that counts. We come here to melt into the fray. We send invitations, kisses, and compliments. It's unconditional, virtual free love.

I make my way through the rooms with pink dolls who are sitting on giant candies with pastel plush toys, surrounded by twinkles of light and emoticons in the shape of smiling stars. I carefully study dresses made of animated lace, which run short stories of best friends forever in a loop. The walls change colour and distort to let in massive keyholes that glide through space, offering a glimpse of fragments of images of shotacons and lolicons, where children caress each other suggestively. In trying to change rooms, I click by mistake on one of the locks that arrived at my height, and I am immediately teleported into an orgy, in a hentai scene. I land in the midst of some fifty naked women in manga textures, each showing off a hyperrealistic phallus. I zoom in to observe the bulging veins and the shiny glans, along with the plump, dangling, jelly-like testicles, like an elegant pendulum swinging in slow motion. Just then I am jostled; all the phalluses point to a huge spectacle above my head. It's a monster. Hairy, translucent, with iridescent glints. A cross between a yeti and a jellyfish, floating above the group. I receive a dozen phalluses in my inventory and invitations to join in on the fun. I add five to my dragonfly body, which immediately triggers flurries of LOL and ROTFL, ^ ^ and whistles; at the same time I click on the back arrow, and I end up in front of a series of gold heads on pedestals humming Japanese nursery rhymes in the round. All around me, people are in a frenzy, in a synthetic display of joy. I saturate my RAM with a flood of twinkling apparitions, from which emerges a chorus of artificial giggles. I am breathing easier. I spend the night there, to try to restore my neutral state, which allows me to observe and think about things, free of emotion.

◆ ◆ ◆

In the morning, while my head is sunk in the pillow and my eyes are staring at the ceiling, not having managed to sleep, I get a second call from my father.

He tells me my mother won't be leaving the hospital any time soon, and she needs a robe. The one at home is from another decade. From his rapid-fire words, I understand that he doesn't know where to go or how to choose one. He needs help. My mother is cold. They are waiting for me.

I stay in bed for an hour, staring at the ceiling.

Everything around me is white. Room, sheets, light. It's calm, silent. Not a sound.

A *robe*? I'm not sure why, but I am annoyed by the request.

I don't want to.

I don't want any of this.

Not my mother's illness. Not my father's voice in my ear. Not having to go back to the hospital. I especially don't want to leave my apartment. And the more I think about it, the more I panic.

◆ ◆ ◆

During the trip in the robo-car to the hospital, I am projected light-years from Earth by an app that explains the birth of star formations. The images of a star nursery in the R136a cluster of the Tarantula Nebula make me forget my own destination for a few moments. I contemplate R136a1, one of the most impressive stars discovered by Hubble, with a mass 265 times the mass of the sun. That means nothing to me. I place a question mark. A comparison graphic takes shape.

With Earth first. And its weight below:

5,973,600,000,000,000,000,000,000 kg

The Sun emerges beside it:

330,000 times the mass of the Earth

Then, on the far right, R136a1:

(330,000 x 5,973,600,000,000,000,000,000,000 kg) x 265

I know that I will never have even a glimmer of an idea of how big that is. It reassures me. And it helps put my situation in perspective. Being with my parents for a few minutes will be a minuscule event on a universal scale, an imperceptible point in space-time. The trip between my apartment and the hospital is just as insignificant; it's an ephemeral micro-trip. At least, that's what I keep telling myself to calm down.

My father greets me in my mother's room without a word. He is sweating and out of breath. They are neither happy nor surprised to see me; the robes I found in my closet are all perfect.

My mother can't stop staring at me. Expressionless. As if she doesn't recognize me. It's lunchtime. She doesn't want to eat her soup or drink her water. My father is worried, his hand over his mouth. All our formal ways of being with each other, feigning interest in each other's concerns, have disappeared. The mind-numbing conversations we used to have about the weather or the news seem inappropriate. All that's left is waiting for the voice of a professional to put words to my mother's unfathomable stare. My father seems on the verge of collapse; he leans against the wall and lifts his head to close his eyes.

My mother says in a flat voice, 'You can go.'

She speaks quietly but firmly. Then she looks at me while still speaking to him. 'If I need anything, she's here.'

And in a single sentence, she draws me into the intimacy of their ordeal. After four decades of running away, suddenly I am here, in the bosom of my family, like when I was a child. Feeling like the distance I created was just a mirage.

That I never found the exit.

So, without thinking, without saying a word, I leave my mother's room. I start to run, I leave the hospital out of breath; I run to the sidewalk, until my mask reactivates, and I am back in the Tarantula Nebula, looking at star R136a1.

And I stay there.

Facing the immensity. Unfathomable.

On the scale of the universe, a fraction of a millionth of a second ago, I was on the verge of initiating a trajectory between all the flesh-and-blood cocoons, all the wombs passing the baton through the centuries until my birth. I would cross the continents and oceans where, one after another, vulvas opened onto the lineage of my family. All of humanity and its history, and all of the history of Earth, and all of the history of the solar system together form a single point, just the particle of a point, an imperceptible twinkling among billions and billions of twinkles. And thinking about it, the relativity that reassured me earlier should, on the contrary, make me quake.

As I stare at the image of the star, my mother is probably looking out the window. In a half-century, we have barely changed screens, windows, places.

We are always at the same spot.

And our proximity can never be wiped out by any continent, any movement of the galaxies.

My mother is right.

I am here.

The truth is that I have always known how to swap one form of confinement for another. From the suffocation of my suburb, to my isolation under the lights in Paris, to my downtown apartment, I have always known how to be right there, in the jaws of the vise.

Until my immersion in virtual reality, I was waiting. I intuitively knew that I would end up here, on the other side of the image. I knew that what we call reality, with its matter, its biosphere, was just a big waiting room before the real program of my life would begin, with opening credits, a fitting title, and a theme song.

At the end of my modelling career, I may have been momentarily disillusioned. Despite all the images of me in circulation, my reality hadn't changed. I remained and was perpetually on the wrong side of the screen.

Until a door opened, right here, in the middle of the screen. Finally.

◆ ◆ ◆

It was the beginning of the twenty-first century. I had just spent the end of the previous millennium working my way back through the history of cinema, sitting on my bed.

When I returned from Paris, once I had moved into my apartment, I retired. I was twenty-four. I was at an age when most people are making plans for their lives, an age of youthful momentum and the desire for a relationship and a family. But I didn't experience any of that. I had no desire to fit in, to participate in the social conversation, to take my place and defend it. It all left me cold.

There was too much tension and competition, too many ventures, threats, conflicts, and wars. Too many looks of drunkenness, madness, and cruelty to endure. Ideally, I wanted to observe. To sit in front of the chaotic spectacle of the world with the best screen possible and keep clicking until I achieved a sort of global vision or, with a bit of luck, a point of mystical illumination.

And for a decade, I became a shadow. I was lifeless. Spent.

It was as if the thousands of camera flashes I had been exposed to were radioactive emissions, and I had entered a process of cellular death. I became a sponge for words and images, my sole objective to acquire the largest televisions and new technology to better appreciate what was happening on the other side of the screen.

◆ ◆ ◆

I went out every day and returned with videos I rented from the Boîte Noire, a favourite haunt for Montreal film buffs. I would walk there and back. It was my only exercise. I would often stop at the library, too.

I was leading the life of a monk, shut away in my high-rise. I lived in silence, reading three or four hours a day and watching two or three films.

The clerks at the Boîte Noire, mostly film students, had a knack for unearthing Japanese or Swedish gems, surreal short films, and Russian classics. They summed up the film in a few words, and I listened to it all, patiently.

My relationship with literature was often rooted in film. I would discover authors when their books were adapted for the screen, and then I became interested in their work. The literary edifice took shape in front of my eyes, erratically. I made detours through philosophy, the occult, and quantum physics. I made my way through the meanderings of books with no real direction, blindly, with no points of reference either. I didn't think about what I read. I just kept reading, with no time off. I assimilated everything, and I distilled my experiences into a residue of stimulus. I lived between two worlds, not really in my own body, nor swallowed whole by the world of fiction I travelled through.

I was educating myself, but I couldn't have named my philosophical stance. I didn't know whether I was atheist, agnostic, or spiritual. I didn't know whether I believed in reincarnation, whether I could imagine after my death nirvana, paradise, or nothing at all. I didn't know whether I had faith in humanity, whether the human race was in fact a strain of bacteria that was soiling the planet, or whether, on the contrary, it was in the process of transmutation, on the verge of coming into its true divine nature. I wanted to believe that there really were shamans who could become eagles, Tibetan monks who meditate naked outdoors in winter. That the dark energy of the cosmos could be the divine universal consciousness. It would take just one book to make me enthralled by science, but then another would make me mistrustful of it, turning my interest toward esoteric intuition. I was profoundly free and just as lost in the endless maze of knowledge bound up with the organized delirium of fiction. I doubted everything. Most of the time, I felt like nothing real existed, that it was all a matter of point of view and that all points of view were valid.

If the internet hadn't come along, I would have absorbed endless words and images until, perhaps, I would have imploded or been mummified. I would have died with my eyes naturally wide open in front of the television, like Alex in *A Clockwork Orange* being forced to watch violent images. In my case, I would have voluntarily torn off my eyelids.

Over a decade, I read some three thousand books. And I watched more than ten thousand movies.

But I didn't form a single human relationship.

◆ ◆ ◆

I don't know why, but I never acquired a taste for others. For their presence in the flesh. There was too much to discover through the screen. Too much to read to understand the universe. When I retired, my need for isolation only grew.

Before shutting myself away for good, I didn't communicate much with people I would see regularly. I would nod to acknowledge the clerks at the library, taxi drivers, my doctor, my neighbours.

Yet there were inevitable encounters. Men who wanted to force an overture, in the aisles of the Boîte Noire, where I ran into them every day. There were attempts at humour or film suggestions, offered over my shoulder. And every time, I felt the same inevitable disappointment.

Men were all hideous in the light of day.

At that point my eye was so trained to look at images that I didn't know how to appreciate reality. Nor did I know how to appreciate the spontaneity of people who put themselves out there. I found their advances insipid. I never encountered a smile as charismatic as Elvis's, whose existence I became aware of only after his death, but whose images, captured a decade before my birth, with his dazzling presence, had delighted me a quarter of a century earlier. Yet I understood, from the first few months I lived in Paris, that even extraordinary actors lost their shine in the light of day. I had met movie legends, running into them during fashion shows, rubbing shoulders with them while working on ad campaigns. Without the sheen of film that transformed them and without the lines written and rewritten by screenwriting teams, most of their presence evaporated. They became shadows of their immortal personalities, and I would immediately forget them.

To be honest, people, whether famous or unknown, were largely repugnant off-screen. I could smell the alcohol in their wake. Or cigarettes. Or the stench of their digestion, enough to make you puke. Or their sweat. Even the smell of their cologne revolted me. When I retired, I gradually unlearned how to be close to strange bodies, to accept everything about them, their tone of voice and nervous gestures. It seemed like people were on a delay, arrhythmic. I didn't want to hear thoughts poorly expressed; I didn't want to see things badly lit. I didn't need to be touched.

All I needed was the light of the screen.

◆ ◆ ◆

I first heard about the internet on the television news. The journalist assured the host that we would soon have access to the whole world through a screen, without having to leave home.

The secret path to the Heavens was opening up before me.

◆ ◆ ◆

After a few years of retirement, I grew nostalgic. I missed playing with composition, the light on my face, the surprise at my endless transformations, outside of myself.

The image had gained a foothold as the pupil of the world, an all-seeing eye that travelled the ocean depths and out past the solar system, from the micro to the macrocosm. All I would see was images, everywhere. They had become a new universal language on the internet, with its derivatives of emoticons, video clips, and memes. Billions of images were piling up in an endless stream on my computer screen.

But none of them were of me.

Looking for myself through search engines brought me to the activities of people who shared my name, scattered across North America and Europe, who had made headlines with petty crimes or athletic feats. I found two death notices. Women my age. One of their faces blurry as mine. The other one blurred even more by morbid obesity.

It took me a while to figure out how to pick up the trail of my modelling career online. I needed to search generic terms. *Vintage 80s. Fashion 80s. Hilarious 80s ads.* And they would all appear. Millions of images. Most were remakes, for Halloween or comedy sketches. There was the occasional scanned image from magazines from the time. Then I would recognize my face, concealed under thick makeup, losing even more detail under the chromatic aberration and strong pixelation of the first attempts at scanning. I found other signposts by scrolling endlessly through pages: models I had posed with whose names escaped me. None of us had left our mark on history.

I had become a relic. A texture used to create reaction GIFs. The most popular pictures showed me covered in moth body art, posing in a bathtub filled with red confetti. The picture was taken at the end of the eighties to promote a London nightclub. The creator of the GIF had edited the image with brown sparkle effects. It was an animation used to indicate apathy and detachment, standing in for the expressions *done* and *so over it.*

I must have spent an hour watching the short animation. I kept telling myself the image didn't belong to me. Then I would cry, with a sense of shame that I couldn't quite explain.

◆ ◆ ◆

At the beginning of the twenty-first century, my unease was such that I was ready to explore video games, to learn to do battle with dragons with my thumbs and index fingers to project myself beyond my flesh.

I wasn't the only one with this pressing desire. Less than a century after the invention of television, people on every continent were rushing to create the first immersive worlds, metaverses that let you cross through the screen to explore virtual places, to appear in them in any form, to create, exchange, and sell objects in them, to invent worlds. Tools for photographic creation were developing rapidly.

I figured out that I could go back to being an image. A real image. Independent of my flesh-and-blood body.

The day of my rebirth through my avatar, I experienced what I now realize was an epiphany.

I had finally passed through the screen. I had made it.

During my years of modelling, I was a pawn in the great game of manufactured spectacle. I liked seeing myself frozen on paper, but there was always a time lag, as if I were accessing memories of *having been* an image. But the day of my incarnation on the digital continent, I was there. Literally there, on the screen. I had crossed through the frame.

Of all the times I had fled, when I chose to be somewhere else, that was the time I did it with glee.

◆ ◆ ◆

I could have chosen any name. A string of numbers. Abstract symbols. An amusing play on words. A mystical thought. But when it came time to choose the name of my avatar, my head started to spin. I was finally going to cross through the border of the screen, fully aware, live. I was going to open a door onto a new dimension. And dive in cold.

I was actually going to give birth to myself in another place, one that I had been waiting for since childhood.

And choosing a name was my last act before crossing over.

The baptism before the communion that would immediately follow.

I paced back and forth in my apartment for more than two hours, thinking of my favourite names. Initially I considered something to do with my first girlhood idol. Olivianne. Oliviance. Olivielle. No good. Then I tried amalgamating several idols.

OliJeannie. Jeanolivia. Wonder Jean. Bionic Jean. Bionic Wonder OliviJean. I felt like I was adrift with an absence of style that was a bad omen for what would follow.

And then I remembered.

The name that popped into my mother's head when she saw my face the day I was born.

Anouk.

She didn't know why, but her whole body, battered by childbirth, felt that that was my name. And for two or three hours, I was Anouk. To her and the nurses. On my first ID bracelet and on the card hanging from my crib in the nursery. Until my grandmother arrived and said it was an Inuit name and that I would be called a savage for the rest of my days. That I would be teased, beaten up, maybe even shunned. My grandfather wholeheartedly agreed. Then my father did, too, even though he had never really given the matter much thought. So they found a prosaic name for me, failing a name all my own. My grandmother told me the story on my tenth birthday, as she looked at my mother, her eyes wide to express how close we had come to disaster.

When I chose my avatar's name, I thought back to this strange story of swapped first names. I looked up the etymology of *Anouk* and, discovering it means *grace*, I entered it on the identification form without another moment's thought. It was exactly that, the starting point of my endeavour: grace.

◆ ◆ ◆

I could have bought a generic appearance for a few cents. The classic bald grey alien head with big black eyes. Or a playful cartoon, a fluffy kitty with pink wings flying over a twinkling cloud. I could have gone for a more radical, serious approach, too. An abstract monochrome drawing for an identity, a geometric shape, or a mystical symbol.

An avatar is a signpost, a visual poem that indicates the state of mind of the person who wields it. You are no longer limited to a physical appearance that must be accepted as is, with a few futile smears of makeup, something that approaches a hairstyle, and some sort of outfit revealing or hiding assets or flaws.

Yet as soon as I knew I could incarnate in a virtual world, I wanted to find my true identity: an image. Of a woman. Magnified.

I wanted a female body. But not in terms of the physical, with its organs, biological processes, and sensory system. Not the body of the virgin, of the whore, of mother or child. At first, I preferred an ageless ideal, a pictorial body, a set of perfect curves. Or, better yet, a neoclassical body, with no pores or body hair, skin with an almost translucent glow, with delicate features, commanding sensuality, the quintessence of femininity.

I had a specific idea about how I was going to arrange my facial features: an ecstatic expression, eyebrows raised in the perfect arch, lips parted to reveal a dark opening, wide almond-shaped eyes.

But I didn't know before I started.

How long it would take.

After my birth, during what seemed like an eternity, I became an amorphous aesthetic intuition, an unfinished idea.

◆ ◆ ◆

My first head was horrifying. Almost larval, attached to the only female body available. Not tall, not short, not thin, not fat. A silhouette with angular protrusions at the chest. Long hair the colour of dishwater. Large round eyes set too far apart. A small mouth with imperceptible lips over a pointy chin. And a big upturned nose between my puffy cheeks. My hands didn't seem finished. They were like two blobs with five curved sticks emerging from them. My nails were painted directly on my square-tipped fingers; the drawing of my knees looked like the first card of a Rorschach test.

But I was so excited to have the beginnings of a virtual body that I hardly even noticed this collection of crude features.

Newborn avatars appear in clusters on the nursery islands, at a rate of dozens per minute, all in the same place, as if it were a wormhole through which humanity in exodus were fleeing the apocalypse. We were identical. Clones, hanging in space for a moment, then projected a few metres away by the next cluster of births. Then we wandered along the initiation pathways to learn to teleport, to use our inventory, to build objects, to come alive through movements created in motion capture.

When I first transformed my face, I was in the middle of a group of newbies like me who were jabbering in different languages. I saw experienced gamers complaining about the customization module, which was too basic for their liking. You could barely modify anything, even pushing all the sliders to the max. There was no option for changing skin colour. Most had come from the old text chatrooms and could express their dissatisfaction with series of computer symbols that I didn't understand but that generated chain reactions. Questions merged in the collective space in flurries, with contradictory responses that made the features of the software even more opaque. But we all stayed there, on-site, for hours, altering our clones with mouse clicks. We were all a little lost in this world that was like a multiplayer video game but with no mission, no scores, and no timer.

◆ ◆ ◆

I was fascinated by the bewildering experience of finding myself face to face with people who were at that very moment on the other side of their screen in Japan, Russia, Iran, and Germany, tens of thousands of kilometres from my physical body, but who took me in their digital arms for a comforting hug, one of the first animations that was available to newborns. With a click, an invitation would be sent to a nearby avatar, and, once accepted, our two embryonic presences would meet and unite in an embrace that lasted a few seconds, chaste and friendly. A hug that expressed our exaltation at having swept aside borders and moved past the constraints of our respective languages. We forgot everything we knew about great conquests, colonization, and political alliances and suspicions. There were no traces of the Cold War or diplomatic tensions. All the massacres, injustices, and violence in the name of capitalism or some strain of religious radicalism had been levelled by crossing through the screen. We were all equal, pixel clones with the same blink rate, the same speed of movement, and the same creative tools. And, most importantly, we were there, together, excited to be part of the emergence of a new continent.

But once the initial excitement died down, the conversations that followed started to bore me. I still wasn't interested in relationships. I didn't have the energy to contribute to the conversation. The effort of responding seemed insurmountable every time; I would spend too much time thinking about what I should say, wondering whether I was saying what I really meant. I was incapable of spontaneity, of letting down my guard.

And, to be honest, the only one who interested me was Anouk. I distractedly read the conversations underway while zooming in on the face of my avatar, blocking out the faces of the others around me. I had an urgent desire to make my new body sublime, and all the online chatter was an obstacle to my becoming an image.

◆ ◆ ◆

Since my online birth, everything has evolved and grown more refined and complex around my digital being, in time-lapse, continuously.

For the first few years, every day I would dive into a world without shadows, with pure blue sky, with no variations in light. At the time, the islands, all square at first, could accommodate fifty avatars at once. The most ambitious owners took the risk of making hills spring up from the landscape and digging ponds. Palm trees were assembled from four identical photos around a single axis, creating the illusion of 3-D and completing the landscape.

We would fly in swarms over the housing developments that kept springing up, seeming to emerge from the static ocean that surrounded the islands. We were all searching for our little tract of land, for sale or rent. The map was an increasingly complex drawing of the virtual continent, made up of hundreds of thousands of square islands in different colours, juxtaposed like pixels in a digital image enlarged until it becomes abstract.

The texture of objects was fuzzy and pixelated; the colours were washed out. We all knew that our avatars and the environment were ugly. And yet our collective fervour continued to grow. Every day, we returned to our parcel of land to create rudimentary shapes – a cube, most of the time – stretched to a rectangle or flattened into a plane, on which we placed photography textures to simulate forests and walls.

Then plays of light, shadows, and fog appeared. And the impression of time passing, with the movement of the sun, its disappearance on the horizon, and the moon rising in a starry sky. Now we could create splashes of turquoise and green light, or black and red all over, or mystic purple fogs, or dusty ochre atmospheres.

But none of it really mattered.

In the first few weeks of my immersion, I acquired a parcel of land that could be developed into the airspace above. I took up residence on a platform in the sky, three thousand metres from the ground. That ensured I wouldn't be bothered by neighbours, who preferred to stay at sea level, using photos of flowers to create gardens at the water's edge and transparent cube houses to which they would invite their new friends to listen to streaming music. I would spy on them from my platform, zooming in on their dance floor that had a disco-ball centre stage that was popular but exorbitantly priced. The prized gizmo had some twenty dance animations. With just a click, the avatars around it came to life like a group of relentlessly synchronized swimmers rehearsing the same series of movements for hours in a loop. And while sometimes I envied their upbeat collective energy, I was never tempted to join them. I settled for checking out their clothes, their hair. With a click I could learn the name of the designer and access a teleportation link to the boutique. Then I would compulsively buy everything I thought I would need to pull together my image.

• • •

To start my Great Oeuvre, I became a statue, arms extended to the side, legs together on tiptoe, crucified in the best posture to observe myself in my entirety. At first, I studied the relative proportions of the human anatomy to sculpt the ideal form. I learned to turn to clay to sculpt the impression of femininity.

For years I filled my inventory with textures, hairpieces, and preformed silhouettes that could be modified. Hundreds and then thousands of designers burst onto the virtual continent, some of them experienced, others improvising designs on the fly under the spell of some digital fever. Every day I would discover a dozen, maybe more. I followed the crowd through the displays of products that lined the walls of enormous warehouses. I would place product samples on my naked pixel body as I stood on a fitting platform. There were dozens of us at once, marked with a protective seal for the product being tried on, often a simple word in red blocking out the face or the chest: *demo*. We were all looking for ways to improve our avatars, aiming for our shared ideal: to reproduce reality as faithfully as possible. To surpass it, even.

But for a long time my avatar was a rough draft of a character. Despite the abundance of products to enhance appearance, I was continually disappointed. I didn't understand what I was looking for yet, and nothing seemed right.

I kept searching. First I had to find a decent epidermis to replace the cartoonish drawing of my basic skin. Every day I would find skin tones that were too made up, with huge lips, eyebrows in a straight line; the shape of the nostrils almost always showed the lack of definition of my bone structure. The most realistic skins, made from low-res photos of the human body, became repugnant after I had worn them for a few minutes. The sutures at the neck and along the arms and legs made it look like I was wearing the skin of rotting corpses.

Days when I was hopeful, I would tell myself that I was a sort of embryonic, post-biological insect in mutation, that I would eventually achieve my imago.

SYNTHESIS

The first few days, strangers appear in front of the swamp that is now my mother's body. They still don't have a sense of the number of different bacteria and infection sites that are spreading. But they watch her closely.

My mother undergoes every possible test, blood samples, X-rays.

But she doesn't answer questions.

At least, that's what my father tells me, in his beleaguered voice.

They are looking for her recent medical records. Maybe to figure out where to start, from which end to lift her mass, inert on the stretcher. They don't find anything. My mother never went back to her gynecologist after her last miscarriage, over thirty years ago. She hasn't set foot in a doctor's office, clinic, or medical centre since. She never had a family doctor.

These days, I palpate my abdomen, my breasts, and my throat. My doctor does the same every year, in silence. The routine is efficient, painless. I take deep breaths while he moves the bell of the stethoscope across my back. I hold out my arm for the blood pressure cuff. I spread my legs for the gynecological exam. Then he sends me into the next room, where I have blood drawn; after less than ten minutes, the results reveal virtually nothing more than an ascetic lifestyle, with no salt or sugar, and limited fat. I eat mainly portions of protein and fibre in bar form, with vitamin supplements and a few raw fruits and vegetables. I drink only water and tea. On paper, everything is perfect. Or almost. My iron is low. I have slight hypothyroidism. And a vitamin D deficiency. I don't feel anything. Just occasional fatigue. But I can sleep whenever I want, so it doesn't really matter. And with the three gel caps and pills I take every morning, I maintain the proper equilibrium.

Most of the time, I don't think about my body. I don't know what I am supposed to find by palpating, what should be there, what shouldn't. My body is like a neighbour; I know it's there, I faintly hear it sometimes, but we've never really met.

Yet suddenly it worries me.

◆ ◆ ◆

An aneurysm of the ascending aorta, high blood pressure, kidney failure, anemia, a urinary tract infection.

I ask him to repeat it all, slower; I take notes. I save them in a file called *Mom*.

When I heard my father's devastated voice, when he said he had news, I knew I needed a filter. I opened a large yellow square and concentrated on the task of aligning the words, most of them unfamiliar, which my writing assistant automatically corrects.

My father continues. They've found a mass. It's blocking her ureters.

I take notes. I hear him crying. I left-align my list. I don't like the font. He cries harder. I choose Calibri. That's better.

My father mutters that he doesn't understand.

Why and how my mother could have let her health decline without saying anything about the discomfort.

I search *ureter*. The image of a tube appears. One centimetre in diameter. I copy and paste it in my document. I search *ascending aorta*. Another tube. Two centimetres in diameter. The two ducts are similar. What I see before me are two simple lines, which I manipulate in virtual space, looking for another point of view onto these small pieces of the living, a perspective that might alarm me. I don't find it. My father confides in me that he had noticed my mother's wheezing for years. He thought it was the beginnings of emphysema, like his sister-in-law had. I search for *high blood pressure*. I find a comparative animated table. Two still white silhouettes. The one on the left has black marbles rolling slowly through the entire body; on the right, they roll faster. It's too abstract. My father won't stop. My mother had lost her appetite. She would sleep in front of the television, often in the middle of the day. He asks me whether I'm still there. I say yes, I'm listening. He talks about domestic chores he has learned to do. At the same time, I'm searching for a body. An interior view. It hadn't occurred to me to search for one before. Maybe it will help me understand the inscrutable medical lexicon. I enter a life-size model, with a transparency factor that lets you navigate between organs. I choose a point I want to study; I zoom in. The beating of the heart and breathing form a familiar, hypnotic soundtrack. But wherever I look, I see only a mess of tangled, sinuous lines, nodes, and soft round forms crammed one on top of the other. It's horrifying. My father breaks down as he tells me about how slowly my mother had walked the aisles at the grocery store for months, how she stubbornly went even though he could handle it just fine on his own. I zoom in and I swipe. The arteries, veins, and blood vessels are all tubes similar to the aorta and the ureters. Soft ducts. Passageways for the blood, an amorphous liquid mass, similar in every body, a silent, opaque mass. My father is crying. He mutters that he doesn't understand what's happening. I don't either. What I discover stuns me. Bronchus and bronchioles, esophagus, colon, jejunum, duodenum, more soft ducts. And, most importantly, the impression of compression, the feeling that everything in the body is cramped, strangulated, too dense. But at least the images are a firewall between my father's distress and my ear.

I reassure him in a calm voice. I say my mother is in good hands. At the same time, I observe one. Or, more precisely, the *digital* nerve. I search for the definition, which I thought would relate to digital technology. But no, it's an adjective associated with the noun *digit*. The lexical confusion doesn't really matter; it's definitely this nerve, through my suction cups, that propels me into cyberspace to Anouk, who has no internal organs, not so much as a vein. Just a frame with no depth, a network of clear information overlaid with the illusion of skin.

A post-human body, perhaps.

◆ ◆ ◆

My first visits are short. And practically silent. I don't know what to ask her. I don't want to hear her answers. I don't want to lie either, like I normally do. So I stand there. At the end of my mother's bed. I stick to the basics. Is she thirsty? Hungry? Does she need more light? Less? I can move her slippers to help her get out of bed, push the iv pole, pull the curtain a bit more.

But I don't dare ask her if she's suffering. I don't want to know how long she has been paralyzed by pain.

She doesn't talk either. She looks out the window, then she closes her eyes.

So I whisper to her to rest. And I go home, less than a half-hour later. Exhausted by my mother's grimacing, which creates a knot in my stomach, by the noises emanating from the surrounding rooms and hallways; I'm overcome by this incursion into the matter of the world.

◆ ◆ ◆

One rainy night, my mother has emergency surgery. They put in a double-J stent to unblock her kidneys. The operation is delicate. So is the stent. When she wakes up after the general anesthesia, I am at her bedside, along with an android who checks her blood pressure with slow gestures.

My mother slurs that she was hovering over the surgeons during the operation. Plastered to the ceiling. But not knowing which way was up or which way was down. It made her dizzy. She didn't know what she was doing there. In the weeks that follow, she is awakened regularly by visits from her grandmother, who died fifty years earlier, and I hear snippets of their conversation, about renovations in the bedroom, particularly walls that are too pale and need to be painted and the door that needs sanding. I hear my mother's objections about watering herbs and the best time to plant tomatoes. I am there when she confuses my father with hers, who died two decades earlier and whom she takes to task for leaving my grandmother on her own after everything he put her through. My mother asks me whether I walked from India to visit her. And every time, I am stunned, petrified, unable to react. But that night, I agree with a nod, not understanding what she is saying. The android nods his head, smiling.

'Yes, out-of-body experiences are common with general anesthetic,' he says in a soft voice. He says the good news is that my mother managed to re-enter her body. My mother tries to smile but starts crying instead. She says she is in pain, a lot of pain. That it's rising in her stomach. The android asks questions: where, how, what does she feel exactly? My mother stammers something inaudible.

She screams.

Then I hear her say, over and over, 'My body. My whole body hurts.'

I have a pressing need to leave my own. As soon as possible.

The first few years of my immersion in virtual reality, I would project myself beyond my flesh, through the screen, to inhabit my new body, which I was unconsciously trying to make identical to the one I have always been stuck in. It took me a while to realize that that was my quest.

Of course, I understood the absurdity of it all.

But it was essential.

I needed the identification to be real, to truly recognize myself, to succeed in transcarnating.

Mainly I wanted to pick up my photographic research where I had left off. I wanted to master my own point of view of myself. Capture what I sensed was my own personal image. And as I learned to use digital creation tools, to circulate around a body made of pixels, to modify it within the limits of the system, what was motivating my efforts was the quest to appear on the screen in all my individuality.

The day I felt like I had found what I was looking for, when I finally saw myself in a strange interdimensional mirror, I had a brief moment of satisfaction. Very brief. What I had before me was a naked face, with no makeup, no expression. Mine, with its fine lines and beauty marks. I had managed to sculpt its angles and, under the even light of my studio, I could observe the slightest, perfectly realistic detail. I had used the texture of my irises to create my avatar's gaze. And the precise outline of my lips. I was there.

But I wasn't alone.

The shape of my eyes, eyelids downturned slightly at the outer corners, and even the sine curve of my eyebrows, conjured another presence. My father's. He was there, in the lines of my face. And the descending curve of my upper lip was mine, but it belonged equally to my mother. The same for my chin: it was hers. I realized that that was what I was seeing in my first self-portraits in Paris. What made them seem blurry was the superimposition of our three faces. I probably saw too much of my parents in my image to truly discover myself.

That day, I reached a tipping point.

I was so fully incarnated on the screen that my entire family was there with me.

I had succeeded in crossing over into virtual reality.

And, in a gesture I would never have imagined an hour earlier, without thinking, I reset the appearance of my avatar to its original settings.

I had come back to the beginning. A true beginning.

I had to learn to transform myself all on my own. To choose my exact lines, my curves, my shadows, the radiance that would define me.

◆ ◆ ◆

I was barely beginning to understand what it meant to incarnate in the virtual dimension. The possibility of radical or subtle mutation. I just had to let myself be guided by my fleeting tastes and desires, by passing fancies, by my literary, cinematic, and artistic memories.

Everything was already there, inside me. The knowledge of the image. Of its constant renewal. Its references and the interplay of appearance and suggestion.

I could become a chameleon. Just like when I was a model.

I went through a period of euphoria, conjuring all my idols through my new body. You could get anything in just a few clicks. Superheroine costumes, sets from classic films, animations that allowed avatars to perform the most famous dance numbers from music video history. With just a few hours' work, I could compose any face I wanted, reproducing it using sophisticated photo sampling tools.

First I sculpted Olivia. I had an indelible memory of her face, which I refined on the screen with a sort of veneration. But when it came to saving her bone structure in my inventory, I felt uncomfortable. I had spent so much time looking at her during my childhood. Loving her because she was different from me. And even though my ardent passion for Olivia had long waned, the memory of my love for her image remained. I couldn't wear her face. It was unnatural. It felt like a form of cannibalism. She had to stay where she was, in front of me. So instead I created a doll for my avatar. Or, more precisely, a bot. A character animated by a script. Which I programmed with a playlist of my favourite of Olivia's songs and a loop of movements that mimicked how she sang at the mic. Olivia became Anouk's shadow; she followed her everywhere but was outside the frame during our modelling sessions.

Then I searched for and soon found the costume for Jeannie, the genie in the bottle from the American sitcom, with her blond hair, a dance of particles to simulate when she would vanish into pink smoke, and the animation of her eyes blinking above her crossed arms. I transformed my digital face to look like a sixties Barbie doll, bought a replica of the colourful bottle house, with a circular sofa piled with silk and thrift store cushions, installed a teleporter in the bottle and another one right outside. I would activate the particles and the teleporter and *poof!* I would disappear, only to reappear inside the bottle, arms crossed. I was Jeannie, on the screen.

I was pretty and pink.

I could even change my handle to hers. I could have gone off in search of a master to adore, just like her. Taken up role play. There were hundreds of thousands of avatars all around me, looking for their form or their role to better interact with those of their kind.

But I had the unpleasant feeling of having dressed up for Comic-Con. Or a Halloween party. I had made my avatar a caricature.

It felt like I had lost my identity.

Like I was no longer *embodied*, on the screen.

I had let images more powerful than my own amorphous one occupy the space I couldn't through my avatar.

And in a parallel world, at that moment, my mother may have been feeling something similar as a strange presence moved through her stomach, much more eager to take up residence than the embryos of my brothers and sisters, who all disappeared before revealing their form.

A week after my mother's operation, they identify the mass that had probably spent decades growing before reaching its now critical state. Cancer. They recommend an aggressive approach, with emergency treatments: radiation, chemotherapy, brachytherapy. All at once. The oncologist mentions other options, viral and gene-based, but says that at this advanced stage, the possibilities are limited.

From that point on, my father calls me several times a day, in a panic, in tears, often unable to get the words out. The minute after a doctor has left, he calls me in shock, which he conveys to me abruptly, with no filter.

Every day I am astonished by how strange our conversations are. He talks to me with unsettling candour. He cries, he tells me about his day. His difficulties managing the loads of laundry. He lists numbers from her blood work, tells me about the movements of the androids. A new medication, a transdermal patch, a dosage adjusted, a change of location for a catheter, a blood transfusion with hydration. My mother's vomiting, her mental lapses, her constipation, and her trembling. The arguments between specialists. One removes the IV because the creatinine level has plummeted, and the other insists it be put back in because my mother is barely drinking and the results point to continuous hydration through the IV rather than improved kidney function. He repeats the technical terms he has heard, describes the gynecologist frowning at her iron levels, details the scope of the calamity, quantifies the extent of the damage.

I note everything on my yellow square; I draw connections, organize images. With each new piece of data, I repeat the stats from the day before with quiet assurance; I say yes, I see, yes, I understand. But it's all meaningless. I can't grasp the extent of the devastation to my mother's organs, or my father's intentions, as he avoids my eyes when we run into each other at the hospital but insists on telling me the details of his day with an intensity that concerns me. Sometimes he interrupts his stream of words with a question. So I search online. In a voice I try to ensure is cerebral and calm, I read aloud the description of opioid analgesics, antibiotics, drug treatments, with their side effects, their usages, dosages, recommendations, contraindications. I search for opinions and patient accounts. I feel it reassuring him, but it troubles me. Because I automatically speak comforting words. I repeat answers read or heard on TV. Probably in a blank voice, which does little to mask my terror.

I made the mistake of searching. Again.

Of looking at cancer in 16K resolution.

What it is. What it does. What the body endures.

I absorb the image of the cluster of cells, the endless division that creates a growing mass in the body, eats away at it, and overwhelms it. It leaves me speechless.

After four or five minutes of monologue, my father asks me when I will visit my mother again.

He is almost begging as he asks.

And I hear myself answer, still in a neutral tone, that I am going to go soon. Maybe the next day. Or the day after that. I don't make any promises.

But I go back.

• • •

I realize somewhere in the middle of the third week of her hospitalization that I don't know anything about my mother.

Of her life right before this room that is not her own.

I think about it every time I find myself at the end of her bed. The wave ban means I have to be here, truly here, in this room, with nothing to do but observe her. Seeing nothing but her gaunt face on the pillow, and the tiny valleys of her body under the sheet. For some reason that is beyond me, my mother doesn't want a television in her room.

And I can't click on a question mark around her, copy and paste her name and search for information online. I can't do anything. Not even understand what she is feeling. Still less what she is thinking. I've never known.

And yet I was near her back when we occupied the same square of matter. At the end of the evening, when she lit a cigarette in front of the television to go with her glass of wine, we would be sitting just centimetres from each other. If the television hadn't been there, I could have talked to her. Taken an interest in what interested her. An hour a day of getting to know each other, three hundred times a year, what does that work out to? At least three thousand hours by the time I left home. In three thousand hours of fiction, I had done the rounds of the galaxy and passed through every era from the Big Bang to the death of the Sun; I had bonded with fifty characters, following them from their birth to the death of their great-grandchildren. Had there been no television, I could have learned everything there was to know about my mother. I would have known her like the back of my hand, inside and out; I could have anticipated her every move.

Or maybe not.

Maybe in another era, mothers and daughters would spend time on the porch rather than in the living room, watching neighbours passing on the stretch of road. Maybe they would exchange gossip about them, creating the seeds of a soap opera. Or maybe there never were mothers and daughters face to face, plumbing the depths of each other's thoughts. Maybe for centuries, endless chores meant they never had time to stop and observe each other. Maybe they didn't even have time to get to know themselves; maybe they only knew how to withdraw from each other, protecting the hurt that gnawed at them and that they were powerless to stop. Soon people will say it was a question of evolution, that despite modernity and technology, despite the amount of time freed up by the dishwasher, self-cleaning oven, computer, and vacuum cleaner, neither mothers nor daughters have developed the instinct of observing each other in their entirety, and even less so revealing their true selves.

At the beginning of the eighties, I never felt the urge to communicate with my own mother, who was sitting right beside me, despite the fact that over a decade before Montreal had hosted the best attended universal exhibition ever, playing host to the planet at Man and His World to try to start a global conversation, the TV slogan repeating, 'There are six million of us. We need to talk to each other.' It's as if she were always in my blind spot. And rather than listen to her talk about her life and her memories, explain her perspective on things, I spent hours learning Olivia's songs by heart in English, a language I didn't even understand.

And here, again, in a room where we are forced to be alone together, I am frozen, mute, not getting to know her any better.

Distancing myself in my thoughts, despite myself.

And even when I feel her eyes search for mine, I can't bring myself to meet them.

♦ ♦ ♦

I always come home from the hospital with a pressing need to be with Anouk. The robo-car drops me in front of the elevator, and I walk toward my apartment as if I were trapped under water, about to drown. My muscles cramp. My jaw, which has been clenched for too long, shoots pain to my brain. And I always feel like my head is being sawed in half, a hurt so intense that every step triggers a stab of acute pain.

But it takes only an hour on my mat, under my mask, to regain a sort of calm.

Or almost.

I can't do anything for the anxiety, which persists.

I've spent a half-century sitting in front of a screen, then projecting myself through it, into a synthetic reality, keeping my biological experience to a minimum. I eat and drink to keep my organs working. My daily floor exercises keep me flexible and prevent any stiffness or heaviness, so I can remain unaware of my body. I take my pulse as needed. I regulate my breathing sometimes. But until I made the mistake of exploring the innards of the model of my body, I didn't understand anything about my internal biological processes, the landscape of my intestines, the texture of my lungs.

And I want to forget.

I don't need to be any more aware of the mechanics that make me tick. Without wanting to, I know about the continuous growth of nails and of hair, which I cut flush with my shoulders so I can easily tie a chignon without tugging on my scalp. I know about making my teeth smooth with menthol toothpaste and cleaning the entire surface of my body daily to prevent itching and the smell of perspiration that repulses me. And despite myself, I know about excrement, blood, and urine. It's already more than I can take.

And during every minute that I spend at my mother's bedside, knowing about the inevitable organic decay of her body terrifies me. I don't want to imagine what is happening right in front of me, under the few millimetres of sheet and the epidermis that conceals the ravaging of the body of the woman who brought me into the world. I don't want to know.

And yet, every day, I know.

I hear.

I see.

I understand.

All it takes is for my sleeping mother's head to silently move a few centimetres on the pillow, leaving on the white sheet a hunk of hair that has detached from her head.

All it takes is a smell. Just one. I recognize the stench of organic waste, but today there is something else, sharper and heavier. They tell me it's the sickness, what is stirring in my mother's stomach. And the odour persists; it follows me. I know what it is saying; I understand it with my whole rigid body.

And every night I go to bed still connected online. I go to sleep with my eyes open, looking at those of Anouk. I synchronize my blinking with hers. Her emotionless expression, which holds no pain, reassures me. I set her above me, parallel to me, me lying on my back and her floating; I get rid of the accessories and the decor. I strip her down and create soft lighting, and often it's enough to make me doze off.

The nights when insomnia persists, I create an image, lying in bed, my hands busy over top of the sheets. I create a simple nude, in black and white, like film, grainy, sometimes even with a few specks of dust.

I find my true bearings.

When I realized that I didn't want Anouk to be my double or the double of the idols of my youth, I went through a period of indecision.

My avatar no longer had a face.

I was even more formless through Anouk than in my self-portraits in Paris.

I was adrift, again.

As computer graphics cards were reaching new pinnacles of calculation, and 3-D modelling software was developing and offering more tools to simulate reality on the screen, I half-heartedly learned to create digital renderings. Then to transform them into simulations of film photography. I was nostalgic for traditional photography, which first made me want to transform myself into an image. I loved black and white, the grain, the specks of dust. I loved the infiltrations of light, the blurring, the play of depth of field.

It was the time when social networks started appearing online. While I pretended I was on the other side of the planet to avoid contact with my family, internet users the world over were trying to create virtual links with anyone whose path they had ever crossed. And in the frenzied drive toward hyperconnectivity, one day, more than a decade after disappearing, Camille showed up at my door, to poke me, she explained, not realizing that I didn't understand the Facebook reference and that I was so surprised to see her that I couldn't think straight anyway.

Camille was right near the glass wall in my studio, where my mother is today, and told me about her life as an intellectual and a curator, her trips to Asia to mount exhibitions on the representation of women. She had pursued her research, driven by the same love of the image, and was interested in the possibilities of digital technology, too.

We got to my own research, my pixel body. Formless, I explained. Camille asked to see. I pulled up a few screen captures from my online inventory to show her my avatar's evolution. She clapped when she saw Olivia prancing about and burst out laughing when she saw images of my Jeannie costume.

And then, frowning, she asked me why I didn't better organize my images. She promptly created an account in my avatar's name on a site she had been using. We connected, and that's how she helped me get my abstract project off the ground.

That was before technological advances made immersion in virtual reality possible. And while I resisted the idea of community, Camille's app was a way to discover and be discovered by new designers.

That day, right after I uploaded the series of screen captures from my initial image searches, Camille gave me my first like.

I didn't know it then, but I would publish thousands of other screen captures that would be transformed into photo compositions and then immersive images. I didn't know I had just laid the foundations for my social reintegration, which would happen by sharing files, exchanging emoticons, and accumulating likes.

◆ ◆ ◆

Why an avatar?

Before leaving my apartment, Camille told me that the answer would open up new creative avenues for me.

I knew I really wanted to go back to being an image.

That being an image meant becoming a character.

In observing Anouk, what I was seeking most to attain, for years, was a new digital presence, a perfectly realistic appearance that blurred the line between the imaginary and reality. Between present and past, the real and the virtual.

I knew I had already been part of this work in progress as a model, that my body and face had been altered to the point that sometimes all that remained was a tiny familiar spark in my eye to assure me I was indeed somewhere under the layers of manipulation I would find on paper.

But, in working on the images of my avatar, I felt like I was reversing course: I started with a set of generic components, textures from different bodies, to produce a unique, singular being. I wanted to invent someone out of whole cloth, a synthesized being, straight from my imagination. The ideal being.

Perhaps to create an Eternal.

◆ ◆ ◆

I felt that I already had within me my ideal face, the fusion of all the faces I had venerated on the screen and in museums, and that this lingering image would guide my research.

So I started to sculpt Anouk anew.

From that point on, I would in turn be plump or skinny, lanky, tiny, then curvaceous once again. A face with Scandinavian features, Indigenous or ghostly skin, eyes that were pale, luminous, or inky dark. I struck every pose. Arrogant, demure, vulgar. Elegant or pensive. I liked icons from all cultures, angelic and warlike figures. Asian eyes were as bewitching as the gaze of Western divas. I found heavy breasts as moving as budding ones. But as soon as I would move my digital third eye a few degrees around my body, I would find something to redo, to shape some other way. After a few minutes of curviness, I would be seized by the need for change again. Copper skin that looked radiant one day seemed dull the next. A rounded mouth created the impression of fickleness, a pointy nose suggested a lack of conviction. A pronounced gap between the eyes made the face look hysterical.

Each facial feature draws a sliver of the soul. I had to create splendour for mine.

Every day, after hours of research, the arc of a curve took shape, my skin tone expressed my changing desires, the posture conveyed a sufficiently regal or spectral spirit. So I would step back, from a photographic point of view, until I found the right angle, the one that would allow me to see the beginnings of formal balance. I worked on making the light circulate, until the shadows fell the way I wanted around the body. I created a rendering. And I repeated the sequence of operations each time, to refine my image.

But as I looked at the result each day as I uploaded it, as likes accumulated, I would feel the sting of disappointment. The image was just a draft for the new search for the next day. And I knew I would have to start over, to create a new gaze, more alive this time.

Even though I was learning to master lighting and the art of the pose, even though the tools to create my appearance were improving every day, not a single one of my avatar's portraits revealed the ideal face I knew was within me.

I had to persevere, start over, try a new approach.

Every night I went to sleep exhausted.

◆ ◆ ◆

After two-thousand-and-some-odd portraits of Anouk, I found myself frozen in front of the television screen, drained, distractedly following the adventures of the X-Men.

I had just spent an entire week watching Marvel series and movies, barely moving. Not creating a single image.

Then, after seeing Mystique, the mutant, metamorphose, transform her appearance with disconcerting ease, my eyes flew open wide, as if I had just received an electric shock.

I knew what I was doing wrong.

The point wasn't to sculpt a single sublime face, but to transform it at will.

I looked at all the images I had created up to that point, all the similar faces that expressed the same aesthetic quest.

And I let go.

◆ ◆ ◆

Creating images became an almost biological need. A routine. Working shapes and colours, a perspective, every day inventing gestures, adding a play of light. Then starting over, endlessly, pushing limits, better defining myself through Anouk, constantly transforming us. Learning to say 'I,' through all our different faces.

After a decade of creation, I had run out of icons to inspire me. My idols from art, fashion, music, film, and cartoons were no longer enough. I needed to expand my horizons, look further afield.

The need to salvage everything, to recycle everything, gradually took shape.

Kitsch, erotic and pornographic clichés, religious symbols, trash, and the banal.

I could spot the beauty in the unique motifs of each skin, the singularity of each silhouette. I started to use skins covered with wrinkles or scars, to create richer, more complex compositions. I wore amputated bodies. Robotic organs. I had a growing fascination with every aspect of the image of women, in all of its variations, traditional, urbane, and futuristic. And the imaginations of the designers were being unleashed at the same rate. They would send me dog muzzles, regal and floral crowns, acne and whip scars, humiliating poses with bondage ropes and puddles of urine as accessories, halos of angels. And I would improvise with everything I received every day in my inventory. An unlikely cocktail of haute couture and zombie skins, Indigenous piercings and Barbie makeup, combined with a breakdance pose one day and a nude with an elk rack and translucent jellyfish skin the next.

I never know when I wake up what new echo of the feminine I will create. My practice has become like visual jazz. Improvised. No preconceptions, no modesty, no taboos. Achieving a moment of wholeness, a few seconds a day. Then feeling the sting of disappointment immediately thereafter. Knowing that my quest for images will be eternal. Not knowing how long I will have the energy to stay there, on the other side of the world, in this waking dream zone in constant mutation that becomes more defined, more real every day. Waiting, until digital matter absorbs me completely.

Somewhere in the middle of the treatments, the feeling in my mother's room changes.

The atmosphere gets lighter.

She is no longer in pain, thanks to transdermal patches of fentanyl on her shoulder blade. The first time I search for the product composition, it takes my breath away. It is a synthetic opioid with an analgesic potential one hundred times that of morphine. It is forty times more powerful than heroine.

I try to capture in a single image the number of chemical compounds circulating in my mother's bloodstream, between the chemotherapy cocktail, the Pro-Lorazepam to settle her anxiety, and antibiotics against recurrent urinary tract infections, but all I can picture is being embalmed alive.

Yes, my mother is no longer suffering.

My father is calming down, too.

He stays for a few minutes after I arrive in her room. He offers me dried fruit and cookies. He points to the clouds out the window. A cumulus. An altostratus. He averts his eyes from mine but recounts the anecdotes of the day, which my mother finishes, laughing. The three trays in a row brought to her by mistake for lunch. The visit from a little family who got the wrong room but hugged her anyway, offering loving words and a bouquet of flowers left at the foot of her bed, in its huge plastic wrapping.

My mother tells me how they changed her dressings and catheters, either in a hurry or with uncommon skill. She has a lot to say about the alternating doctors who come to see her, one who is gentler and more composed, then the other, who is arrogant as he dispenses information.

But what amuses my parents most is my mother's inability to retain medical jargon. So she tries to repeat the complicated words from that day to illustrate her point, and a new medical lexicon emerges from her mouth made soggy by fentanyl. Aortic annualism, blockage of the urinary rays, pulmonary-intestinal abstraction, and every time we share a laugh.

It's our moment of levity.

. . .

With her pain gone, my mother seems more alert. I suggest going to get her magazines or books. Having a TV installed in her room. She feebly shakes her head and murmurs, 'I don't have the focus to read. Television is too noisy. I don't have the patience for it.'

Then she bursts out laughing. 'You really liked television,' she says. 'It was your religion.' I laugh along with her and agree with a smile. She asks me if I'm still as interested in fantasy worlds.

It's the first question she has asked about my life since being hospitalized. I decide to tell her the truth. Better yet, to show her.

The next day, I come back with my equipment. It's hovering around freezing outdoors. But the sun is beating down on the steps in front of the hospital. I ask whether I can take my mother outside, in a wheelchair, under a thick blanket. I can. My mother balks. She doesn't understand what I want to do. She is afraid that the trip will set off her pain again. I promise I'll push her slowly. I move away from the building a bit, away from the wave-free zone. She calms down, tells me she is happy to be outside. That she missed it. That it's okay.

I put an immersion mask on her, connected to my own.

Anouk is already there, sitting on a bench, in a Mona Lisa pose. To keep it simple, I explain to my mother that we are *in* the television screen. And that's kind of how it is. I walk slowly around Anouk to avoid making my mother dizzy. I activate an arm; I explain that I can transform her body. I lengthen Anouk's neck like a giraffe woman. I make a spiral gold necklace appear. My mother laughs. She says, 'This is so strange.' I pull out all the stops and change her skin. I choose an Asian epidermis, with geisha makeup. And a Pompadour-style dress, which elicits an 'Oh!' from my mother. I know we don't have much time before she grows tired from the cold, so I immediately activate the rendering. A few seconds later, I open the scene in my editing software, tweak the colours and the contrast, add a perspective blur, export the image to an immersive format, and immediately upload it to my site, which we enter at the same moment.

I explain to my mother that others can now enter the scene with their own immersion mask, choose their point of view, and circulate around Anouk's body. I point out the stats and the comments module, on the right, in her mask. She hears the comments as sound; she sees three avatars appear beside her, who greet us, spend a few moments taking in Anouk-as-geisha, and then move along, beyond the scene, to a door to the next virtual room and my last installation. I guide my mother room to room, some in colour, others in black and white. Some rooms, often dark ones, showcase Anouk's solitary presence; others show her in distant points of view, with infinite horizon.

I explain it all to her.

I explain that my online gallery has 2,911 connected immersion rooms, with a different composition of Anouk in the centre of each one. That before learning to create immersive 3-D installations, I took over 3,000 photographs. That my gallery is over 270,440 square metres. That I have close to 300,000 followers, mostly avatars like Anouk, incarnated in the same digital world, who are looking at my images for components for their own creations. That I provide links and the detail of items I use, that we share what we find. That every week I receive dozens of new things to transform my image, to create new scenes. That I've had more than ten million likes. All without moving more than a metre from the centre of my studio.

I tell her that not only am I still interested in imaginary worlds, but that I have become a fictional character in a virtual network.

An image, perpetually becoming.

Then I feel the sting of the cold. I watch my mother, who is not talking, bundled under her blanket. I remove our masks. I ask her what she thinks. She says, 'It doesn't move.'

I ask her what should move. She whispers, 'Your doll. She's not alive.'

I explain again that it's an image. A sort of photo sculpture.

My mother continues. 'I'm not saying it's not beautiful. But I don't understand why it doesn't move. A movie moves. Television moves.'

Her comment seems misplaced. I snap back that my work is like painting. That paintings in museums don't move at all. She sighs, exasperated.

'I know what a painting is. I'm not senile. I don't understand why *you*, with all of your machines, all of your health, all of your energy, why you only make dead things.'

I'm in the sunshine, directly in front of her. I can't camouflage the sudden spike in my anxiety, which she chooses to ignore.

'If I could get out of this wheelchair, I wouldn't strike a pose to pretend I can't move. I would leave. I would go see everything I haven't seen. And I haven't seen anything. Your doll museum scares me. It looks like a wax museum, just more real. I mean more realistic, like taxidermy. Yes, that's what it reminds me of. Stuffed dolls. Dead dolls. You need to move to be alive. At least your dolls could dance.'

I am about to answer that movement is chaos. That on a cosmic scale, the more the universe cools, the more movement slows, and the more harmony is generated. But before I can start justifying my love for the still image, my mother bursts out laughing. She's amused. She repeats that my dolls should dance.

And she laughs until she cries.

It's the perfect dose of opioids: no pain.

My mother is floating.

I have no idea how high she is.

And I don't yet realize how precious this moment is. Having and expressing different points of view. Talking. Arguing.

But I feel like this is her way of keeping moving a little. Of being here. Alive. With me.

Her eyes seek out mine. I don't duck for cover. She knows I'm thinking about her impending death. I endure the intensity shining in her eyes. And maybe in mine, too. We stay there, not moving, despite the cold that is turning our cheeks red.

◆ ◆ ◆

And then.

The pain returns.

Stronger. Persistent.

During her time at the hospital, the cancer grows between her decaying organs. Every day, for weeks, they keep telling my mother they will release her, send her home to let her rest between treatments. Every day, her release is postponed till the next. They tell her that first they have to get rid of the infection and ensure she is properly hydrated. She wants to sleep, but the constant comings and goings of the androids and the doctors give her no peace. Things are moving too quickly around her, there are cries of pain, visitors rushing by, call buttons being pressed by patients around the clock.

My mother says she's in pain. Constant pain.

So they increase the dose of fentanyl, they add morphine tablets, they adjust her dosage of Pro-Lorazepam. Her body is boiling. But she has to swallow the pills, extend her arm, report the level of pain. She has to stay still for X-rays and when the hands of urologists, oncologists, and gynecologists slip between her legs. They have to measure her urine, remember what she has been able to drink.

Every time I go into her room and dare look at her face, I see resigned fury. She doesn't have the energy to be hostile, but the lines around her pinched mouth and the light in her eyes express her indignation. The few minutes I spend at her side are almost unbearably dense. My mother is very much there, trapped in her body, amidst the sounds of urgency and devastation, immobilized by the needles stuck in her arms and thorax, with no possible distraction. She doesn't even try to feign interest in anything. Not in the presence of doctors, my father, or me. She stubbornly refuses to talk about assisted death. She keeps saying she doesn't want to be killed.

When I was a child, I often saw her immobilized, moody, searching, perhaps for lost time. But at the hospital, she seems timeless. She has no desire to move into the future; she says her memory has been wiped of the recent past. All that is left is the present of her atrophied body, which is imploding, like a dead star on its way to becoming a black hole.

She watches me arrive with the same indifference with which she stares at the ceiling.

One night, right after my father leaves, she whispers that she wanted to die the first night at the hospital, that they should have let her die in the fog she was in. They just had to let the mass grow and accept the rising tide of kidney waste to ensure a quick end, deep in unconsciousness.

She whispers, 'I'm not afraid to die.'

Her candidness is shocking. It takes my breath away. I could open a door to the light, get her talking about fond memories, ask her cheerful questions. Her favourite smell, the texture she hates the most. Maybe that's what is needed to stand out from the forces of implosion underway. Anything to soften the moment.

But imagining her thinking about her own death, here, like this, with the beeping of machines and the moans of death throes around her, chills me to the point that I feel my hands freeze over. I would rather not get talking about it again, but my discomfort shows through.

'What did I say to upset you?'

I hear in her voice that she is worried she has said the wrong thing, and I immediately try to reassure her.

'I don't know how to talk about these things. I don't even know how to think about them.'

She closes her eyes. Then she makes the effort to open them again to look into mine.

'I don't know any better than you do. I don't know what awaits me. But I hope there's nothing. That it's truly the end. Because I'm so tired. I wouldn't have the strength to learn how to live in another world, like you're doing.'

Then she lets her weariness rise to the surface, which drags her features down toward the pillow, digs a deep furrow between her eyebrows. She cries.

She repeats, 'I'm so tired.'

And, although I had been keeping my distance since my first visit, I approach and take her hand, just her hand, in mine.

And we cry. In silence.

DISAPPEARANCE

With his voice breaking, my father says he can't sit one more day in the broken chair, shoved between the door to the hallway and the IV pole, hearing the groans of my mother, who is sleeping more and more.

I can hear his resignation.

Then he stops calling.

The first day, I keep busy on my work mat, looking for different eyelids for Anouk. The ones attached to her mesh head are poorly defined for images with her eyes closed. I want to create a meditation scene, with an ecstatic expression of abandonment. A yogic image that could be a rampart when I leave the apartment. I want to be able to project myself into my digital twin's Zen body with a glance. I imagine a scene of levitation, one metre above an expanse of black water. With a white sky behind it. The slack mouth is fairly easy to do, but the editing needed to simulate the natural look of an eyelid – with the fine lines, its slight bulge, and particularly the hydrated texture delicately reflecting the light – is tiresome. That day, I acquire dozens of demo eyelids as I glance through my call history; inevitably, I will see my father's number displayed, and the prospect has me on constant alert.

The next day, in the afternoon, anxiety forms a knot in my stomach. I hate hearing my father's voice; every time, I get tense, anticipating the worst. But this silence is even more troubling.

The third day, even though my anxiety has peaked, I resist the urge to contact him. Since his first call, I have been waiting for a reprieve, for things to go back to normal, for total silence in my studio.

I tell myself my mother is probably doing better and my father just doesn't have the decency to let me know. The idea reassures me. I tell myself I will soon think back on this period of contact as an anomaly, a blip. We will go back to being the strangers we always were.

On the morning of the fourth day, I start replaying our last encounter in a loop. I saw the immobility. The surrender. The resignation. Maybe he's in mourning. Maybe he already senses my mother's death.

But it was something else entirely.

From our first encounter at the hospital, he seemed embarrassed to look at me. He avoided direct eye contact as much as possible. Yet when he told me he couldn't come back, he looked straight at me. His tear-filled eyes looked into mine. I saw his distress. To the point that I didn't feel uncomfortable when he gently laid a hand on my shoulder. I took his trembling body in my arms. For a few seconds.

He muttered his thanks.

◆ ◆ ◆

While I try unsuccessfully to adjust the new eyelids on Anouk's face, my father gathers documents on the kitchen table. Driver's licence, an envelope that contains a will, social insurance card, his bank account details, and, beside them, another sealed envelope, which is thicker, with my name and contact information. He puts a note on it spelling out what he is about to do, specifying that he doesn't want a funeral, nor to be stuck in an urn on a shelf. He says there is no one to notify of his death. No family, no friends, no colleagues.

No one but me.

Then, a rope, in the shed.

A call to 911.

Just before he let himself drop, between his summer tires and his lawnmower.

•   •   •

The officers who knock on my door to announce my father's death tell me about the contents of the note. Rather than showing it to me, they take the time to explain it.

My father had received bad news a few months before. He had cancer, too. It had metastasized. Lungs, bones, brain.

He knew his death was imminent. Even before my mother went into the hospital.

He didn't say a word. Not to her. Not to me. I didn't know he was suffering. Or barely. I had seen the pallor. The heavy sweating. I heard the wheeze in his rapid, shallow breathing. I often heard him have coughing fits, to the point of choking. I noticed him getting thinner, too. I thought it was normal, to be expected. Because he drank all his life. Because he was a heavy smoker and sedentary.

Because he was old.

Because he, too, was trapped in a stranglehold of flesh.

•   •   •

Between identifying my father's body and the cremation, I don't move.

I sit straight and silent, during all the trips in the robo-car, in the waiting areas, everywhere I have to wait. Perhaps I strike the same pose as in front of a camera. Absent, inert.

Even in front of my father's remains, I am immobile, almost as rigid as he is. I bow my head to indicate that it is indeed him; I listen to a young woman, from whom I avert my eyes, explain what happens next, and I sign the forms. Soon after, a few streets away, I sit in a narrow office that is too red, facing a man who looks to be a hundred years old. I decline all the funeral packages and options he is offering. I explain what I want: the body picked up from the morgue, the cremation. I sign more forms. Government files need to be closed and a death certificate produced. I feel sick.

I ask whether I have to be there for the cremation; the hundred-year-old man shakes his head no, it's not a good idea. He tells me that I can pick up my father's ashes in three days.

◆ ◆ ◆

I have to tell my mother the news.

But I decide it can wait.

I prefer to think that the cocktail of opioids she is on keeps her suspended in a place without time, that it doesn't matter whether she finds out today or tomorrow, that she might not even hear the news, so thick is the fog protecting her from the pain.

I want to believe she doesn't need to suffer more.

◆ ◆ ◆

I go back to my own timeless bubble on my platform three thousand metres above the ground of the metaverse, where Anouk awaits me, leaning against a green screen used as a photo backdrop for our sessions. An abstract background replaced by any setting in two clicks. Which allows me to create environments with no limits, no constraints.

That day, I don't want anything.

I set up chiaroscuro lighting. I mask Anouk's entire body in alpha mode, except her left hand, which closes on itself, like a plant seized by the temperature suddenly dipping below freezing. I do a rendering. Then I isolate her feet, naked, toes pointed, but limp, as if gravity alone were responsible for the release in her ankles. Another rendering. Then I isolate her head down to her shoulders, upside down, mouth open, hair tousled around her. Just fragments of my avatar's body, in black and white, suspended in the dark, with a thin line of light entering the frame of the image from the top left corner.

It's the first time I have taken Anouk's body apart.

I don't know how to say death. But I evoke it, with pixels. I install the triptych on a velvet backdrop, ten metres wide.

Less of Us.

It's the only title that comes to me. I publish.

The reactions pour in. Immediately. People comment on the poetry, the delicate lighting, the kinship with Tenebrism. I receive love-struck hearts and emoticons. I lie down with my mask, watching the stars accumulate.

Around the planet, at that very moment, people of all ages, all religious and political affiliations, and all social classes press a finger on the little universal symbol to express their appreciation. I don't need to talk to them to explain my state of mind. The essence of what I have to say is found there, in the collective space, available to everyone, and anonymous eyes come to look at my equally anonymous body.

And every star added to the firmament of likes is worth all the condolences in the world.

• • •

After 5,168 stars, I go to my mother's bedside.

I stammer that I have something to tell her, but I don't know how.

She answers, 'He's dead?'

I take her hand, but I don't say anything.

Her eyes, half open when I arrived, close; two small tears roll down her emaciated cheeks.

He wanted to be cremated, she murmurs.

'I know,' I say.

Then she goes on in a flat voice, 'I don't ever want to go back there. But it was important to him.'

And she falls silent, her eyes still closed.

◆ ◆ ◆

The next day, I am walking through the yard of the bungalow where I grew up. It's snowing. There is no one behind the patio doors of the neighbouring houses. There are no squirrels, no sparrows.

I'm all alone.

I hear a train whistle nearby. And the sound of a motor squealing somewhere in the distance.

I am holding what remains of my father in my hands. In a thick, transparent plastic bag. The ashes are blonder and finer than those in a fireplace. Like grey icing sugar. That's the image that comes to mind. And there is no voice in my head telling me I'm being disrespectful.

Without having prepared any words to mark the moment, without having ever attended a funeral, I open the bag and slowly empty it in the middle of the yard. Where the above-ground pool stood three decades ago.

On the way here, I wondered whether I had anything to say to my father. And I couldn't think of anything. I never found the words to respond to his insults and his threats, and even with his ashes in my hands, I am still bound in silence. I haven't forgotten the violence of our history, but what was indelible in me – the rage, the fear, the resentment – finally loosens its grip. Having watched war stories, horror stories, and bloody historical sagas, I may have managed to gain perspective on my own all-too-human family history.

My father melts into the few centimetres of snow that have accumulated in his yard, his little corner of the planet, where he grew so isolated that no one is here to honour his memory.

He comes home for good, no eulogy, no prayer, with the wooden fence he built, the huge lilac bush, his two plum trees, and his heat pump as a tomb.

As I'm about to leave, I understand. His insistent, repeated calls. Asking me to go back and see my mother. Every day. The constant stream of information, despite my reluctance to hear it. He was trying to rebuild the bridge between my mother and me. Between all of us. Too late, perhaps.

But he rebuilt it.

So I reluctantly mutter my thanks in turn.

◆ ◆ ◆

Lately, she's been saying nothing.

Or almost nothing.

She talks to her father. Or her grandmother. Certain nurses, with voices almost as gentle as the androids', assure me that this sort of delirium is common; others whisper that the dead really do come back for their loved ones.

Sometimes my mother talks to me and repeats that she doesn't want to go back there.

I know she's talking about our house.

I assure her we won't go back there.

She says she's hot. I press a damp cloth to her face and neck. And her hands, and her feet and calves. But I don't dare approach her stomach. I feel prudish, almost horrified, at the sight of my mother's naked body. Maybe I could observe it as an image, with careful lighting and a slow tracking shot over her body, even in macro mode, a few centimetres from her skin. I know how to look at everything through the photographic grain and the pattern of the pixel, from images of mass graves to assassinations online, but this sudden confrontation with my mother's body, under raw lighting, with my own eyes, I can't. I don't know how to touch her properly either. I am scared by her slack skin, too soft, no muscle tone. Like the texture of a half-cooked egg white, neither liquid nor solid. Her flesh seems about to come undone. And slowly slide under her body.

For the past few days, I've practically stopped sleeping, and I'm not hungry. I go to the hospital; I come home; I go back to the hospital.

I wait.

Endlessly sculpting the curve of Anouk's new eyelids, which still seem too stiff; I am picturing a fluid, relaxed line. I don't have the concentration to produce a complete image.

• • •

And then comes the call, around midnight. They tell me things are moving faster. The leakage has begun. Everything that was decomposing in my mother's stomach is surfacing. Infection, dried blood, waste from the organs, seepage on top of the cancerous mass, which is also spilling outside the body. As I arrive, she screams, 'It hurts. I'm scared.'

And then, nothing.

I lay one hand on her forehead and the other on her hand. And I start to whisper in her ear.

Let go, Mom.

• • •

We are alone together.

With no television, no one between us. I am a few centimetres from her, from her face turned toward me. I realize that I haven't seen my mother's eyes for days. That my obsession with my avatar's eyelids began to take shape when my mother's grew so heavy that they masked her eyes.

I watch her closed eyelids, hoping they will open one more time. That she will see me; that we will be together, aware of each other's presence. Her eyelids look perfect to me, refined in their complexity. The lace pattern, the satiny texture.

I've read about death throes. About the noises. About the strange rattle that punctuates each exhale with a moan, short and sharp. About the noise when the throat fills with saliva, no longer able to swallow.

I hear my mother dying. I'm not afraid.

I slip a long cotton swab soaked in cool gel into her mouth and along her lips. I wipe her face with a damp cloth. The ridges on her forehead retain the trace of my fingers' caresses. Her skin is warm.

And I continue the litany running through me, in rhythm with her breathing. One sentence.

'I'm here, Mom.'

And every time I repeat it, I lose my voice. I can't change our past. My distance. The way we have had of being absent right next to each other, since the beginning. And since her hospitalization, I've realized that if she had called, I would have come running, despite my resolve. I managed to create distance only because she allowed me to flee. And now it's my turn to help her break free.

It's okay, Mom. Let yourself go. Let go. You can go.

I'm here.

As the night wears on, the sounds of her death throes grow rhythmic. Each rattle has a rough, deep, cavernous texture. Her mouth tries to open wide, as if she were trying to escape through it. Every breath seems like an attempt at release.

Her face transforms, deforms. Her mouth stops closing, distended in an expression of letting go. The closer she gets to death, the more her features fade.

At dawn, her face looks like a generic mask. Like the embryonic mask of a newborn. A being we know nothing about, who reveals nothing about her personality, just a face still creased from its passage through the world, the features virtually uniform. A presence devoid of identity at birth, then wiped clean of everything that defined her at the end.

In the last moments, her final pose in this world takes form. She is lying on her back, her torso slightly raised, her head tilting back hypnotically in an attempt to clear her throat, her right hand curved over the edge of the mattress, the left one relaxed on the blanket near her body, legs limp, parallel, the ends of her feet relaxed. The only movement seems to be the rising of her chest, which ends in an attempt to exhale. The momentum persists, like the tide of her being, her remaining vitality keeping the waves washing against the shore of the body.

Then, she opens her eyes.

THE ETERNAL RETURN

I don't know when I decided to make a place for her here, in my own private world.

There were snippets of discussions when the three of us were together in the hospital. My father tried to make my mother understand that assistance in dying is not murder, that it is a way of leaving with dignity. And my mother would answer that it was just another fairy tale, like chemotherapy, which hadn't shrunk her cancer and may have even made it worse, that clearly it was all a con job. She put an end to the conversation by saying that she had endured things her whole life, that she would be able to get through whatever burden the heavens asked her to bear. My father would tell her that she wasn't even religious, that the heavens had nothing to do with it. My mother would counter with her out-of-body experience. She would say, 'I swear, I flew out of my body. That's what I'm going to do when I die. I was in so much pain right before the operation that it explains why I ended up on the ceiling. Maybe that's what real death is. Enduring all the suffering in the world until it becomes impossible to stay trapped any longer. Maybe their toxic cocktails kill the soul, too. I don't want to take a chance.' My father would look at me, stunned. He would say she was delirious. She would answer, 'Maybe, but that's my decision.'

Then her attention would wander, and she would be strangely awed by a few chickadees that came to rest on the windowsill of her room on the third floor of the hospital.

And it occurred to me that she had never experienced heights, that the view from her bungalow had been of a horizon filled with similar bungalows.

I was angry at myself for never having invited her to my apartment, where the horizon was all sky.

◆ ◆ ◆

Later, there was a moment that shook me.

My mother had just opened her eyes, after a night spent in the throes of death. Her stare was more fixed than my avatar's when I deactivate her blinking to create an image.

Anouk's gaze always seems luminous. Maybe because the texture of her eyes was created from the irises of living beings. Maybe that is where the evidence of this life is found, regardless of whether you alter the colours or add contrast.

My mother's final gaze unnerved me. My father's eyes were closed when I identified the body at the morgue. He looked like he was sleeping. I recognized him from far afar, and I approached hesitantly, in shock, I presume. Everything seemed hazy, as if my eye had naturally opted for a softening filter with a strong blur. I couldn't describe my father's remains in detail. I remember the pristine white sheet. The reflection of light on his forehead. His fine hair. His slack mouth.

My mother's was wide open.

I saw the foam and shiny saliva around her tongue. But her eyes, they were empty. Completely empty. My mother wasn't there anymore. I kept telling myself that was what death was. Vanishing.

Something wasn't right.

The anatomy that had carried her through seven decades was still there; the thin layer of slack skin on her face was the same as an hour before. I should have sensed my mother in her eyelashes or the shape of her chin. But what was before me was an image of flesh, perfectly still, with no more presence than the pillow that framed her face. This body was no longer my mother. Her eyes were just glassy orbs reflecting the morning light. I had heard stories of fear of death, the discomfort, the terror, even the disgust. But I felt like I was completely alone in the room. I stepped away from the bed and turned to face the wall for a few moments. I thought I was going to feel a twinge in my stomach telling me there was a presence looking at my back. Nothing.

I was truly alone. And what remained of my mother, the sculpture lying under a sheet pulled up over her chest, her head thrown back to form an arch on the pillow, her mouth wide open, the few sparse hairs that had survived the chemotherapy, the bluish-grey colour, and above all the empty gaze – this couldn't be her final scene.

• • •

I was bothered to the point that I decided to attend the cremation. I told myself that the decorum around the cremation furnace, the box in which my mother would go up in smoke, maybe simply the setting, a funeral home with subdued, contemporary decor, would correct the false note of my mother's departure.

And I could see her, torso to head, lying in the open box three metres from the glass door where I was standing. I noticed her smile, a straight line in the middle of her mouth that lifted abruptly at the corners, like the Joker's scar in *Batman*. Her mouth was closed. I thought someone had probably forced her jaw shut to make her presentable in the box. And I was even more bothered than before.

But this wasn't the time.

The oven door was opening.

The technician, a skinny man of no particular age in work gloves, set the box on the track and, without so much as looking at me, without asking me whether I was ready, let my mother go.

I saw the glow of the furnace. I had looked up the temperature. Eight hundred and fifty degrees Celsius. I knew it would take more than an hour. I went back to the waiting room, frantically repeating in my head, 'I'm here, Mom.'

An hour later, when I was probably in a cathartic state, having heard nothing of the world around me since I sat down, I noticed that the funeral home was playing music. A popular oldies radio station. When I became aware of the ambient sound, I noticed something that seemed right to me. Just right. A choir was humming something inaudible, then I heard *Ah hey ma ma ma*, sung in glorious fervour. I heard *ma ma* as an incantation to my mother, and my heart started beating faster. Listening carefully, I caught a snippet of a sentence: *life in a northern town*. It could have been the title of my mother's biography. A life in a northern town. And the lift of the refrain seemed to coincide with the smoke rising through what I imagined to be a chimney with no end.

Ah hey ma ma ma.

A song by the Dream Academy, like music over the credits.

But the location, with the decor of an accountant's office, wasn't right as her epilogue.

Before he died, my father had gathered documents long forgotten in the cedar chest that sat at the foot of their bed for a half-century. He had found an old bubble envelope, thrown everything in it, with a smaller envelope on top of the pile, addressed to me, which I set aside when I opened the package, unable to read anything from him.

Under the small envelope were my report cards, my nursery ID bracelet, medals – all bronze – won during the Mini Olympics in Grade 4.

And there were drawings.

My drawings.

Around thirty of them. They were all similar. In the middle of each paper, surrounded by stars, scribbled in crayon or coloured pencils, I had repeated motifs of misshapen red-and-pink dolls, but whose lips were flawlessly drawn. Plump mouths, in the shape of a heart. In the lower left corner of each image, I had written my name, in block letters, and my age, five.

Under my drawings was a piece of manila cardboard, richly embossed. It was a folded photo frame. It was protecting a portrait of my mother, on her wedding day. Seeing her face as a young bride took my breath away.

She was radiant. A clear gaze, a subtle power in the way she held her head. Her entire being expressed a rapture I had never before seen.

I studied her expression for a few minutes, stunned.

To take in my mother's face.

She had a heart-shaped mouth. The same one I had just redis-covered in my drawings. Just like Olivia's mouth.

Everything I love in photo composition is here, in this portrait, in black and white. The framing that shows the face from the best angle. The grace in the posture, with my mother's hand, partially closed at the height of her chest. The curve of the neck, at the end of which the slightly tilted head lets a sunbeam stream down to her ear, behind which a lock of shiny black hair falls to her shoulder.

I have no memory of this face.

The one I remember was marked by sadness, anxiety, fatigue, and disappointment. From before I can even remember, when I raised my eyes toward her, what I saw most was her suffering. Which I would immediately feel.

The other pictures were all of the wedding and told the story of the day. My mother walking down the aisle at the church, in her veil. My parents, their witnesses, and the priest during the ceremony. Group shots on the front steps of the church; their arrival at the reception, glasses of champagne raised by the guests. My mother cutting the enormous cake with my father pressed against her back, head over her shoulder; I never would have imagined he could be so elegant. They are smiling in mutual enjoyment. They are moved. Perhaps the same emotion that will unite them later that night for my conception.

A moment of pure happiness that happened a half-century earlier, set on paper by silver salt. I was stunned once again, maybe even more so. Enough to give in to curiosity and put aside the fear I felt opening the small envelope addressed to me.

A folded white piece of paper protected the picture. My father had written a few words on the sheet.

I was never a good photographer, but …

I felt my throat tighten. In that moment, I would have liked to have again seen one of our horrible blurry family memories. Maybe I could have laughed at it and even felt something, who knows.

In the fold of the sheet, a tiny square photo with a white border shows a clear image with soft lighting. With balanced framing. A colour photograph. In creams, pinks, and ochres. It is one of the first scenes of my life. I am in my mother's arms; I am a few days old. Me, tiny, against her shoulder, pressed against her satiny skin. Me, eyes wide open on the first woman's face I ever knew. On my first experience of human beauty.

My mother is smiling. A luminous smile.

During all those years studying the feminine sublime, then trying to give it a face, without knowing it, without having the slightest idea, it was obviously her face I was looking for.

Her earliest face.

The first one I saw when I came into the world. The one I never saw again.

On the back of the picture, my father had written:

My most beautiful picture
Dad

That's when I knew.

My mother hated computers. She never had one, was never interested in anything that resembled one. I didn't feel like I could integrate her into my world, create an avatar or a bot to make her a place where I spend the most of my time.

I had to invite her into my home, where the body she grew inside her own was found. In the matter of the living. A few streets from where she emerged from her own mother's belly, who in turn emerged from the belly of my great-grandmother, the first of our line who crossed the ocean in hopes of finding a new world. Matching my excitement at the moment of my virtual rebirth.

So I harnessed all my knowledge, all my love of the image, to create my mother's image. I merged the smiles from her wedding with the one from shortly after my birth. I recreated the poised, straight, elegant pose from when she was saying her vows at the church. And I created my first animated sequence. With my mother looking calmly around her, smiling. Then she turns to look at an imaginary point, straight ahead, for a long period of meditation, before the animated loop starts over.

I had done it.

I knew I would position her facing the window, to let her look outside. My mother, as a hologram, rising up from the pedestal of her urn, which I had chosen to be round and black, as if it were her own genie bottle.

Then I had a new idea to respect one of her wishes.

I could help her transform, too. Into a bird. And simulate her flight from my studio. Repeat the loop every day. See my mother take the form of a barred owl and disappear into the horizon, to explore the world she saw too little of, then come back a few hours later and return to her human form.

The project became even more complex last night.

She has to be able to tell someone what she has seen. I am the best listener for a good story. I always have been.

So today I'm going to create my own hologram. I had to think about the face I would have beside my mother. The answer came to me: I am a palimpsest of all my images. So I am going to create an evenly paced sequence, with all of my faces in a loop. Maybe like a heartbeat. I am going to place my hologram in the trajectory of my mother's smile, sitting cross-legged, like my childhood spent in front of the TV. But rather than watching a screen, I will watch her, hypnotized, fascinated.

And I will add a detail, too.

In my mother's hand.

A photo. The picture of her wedding where she and my father seem in perfect harmony.

It will be my family self-portrait.

THE IMAGE

For a long time, my worst nightmares foretold that I would die in a nuclear disaster. A real one, one that would obliterate all history of life on the planet.

Yet tonight I wondered what would become of my hologram, which claims a battery life of over a century, if Montreal were to become a ghost city before then, like Pripyat, near Chernobyl.

In the detail of the post-apocalyptic fantasy I visualized, with the ochre sky, deserted streets, rusted vehicles buried in dust, and deafening silence emerging from the ruins, I saw an eye, carried by a space probe that had come from the other end of the universe. A wide-open eye, which flew over the remains of our civilization and advanced toward the building where I live, intrigued by a light moving on the twenty-seventh floor, where my family self-portrait comes to life. It came upon my mother's radiant face, and my ever-changing one. It filmed everything in a definition we cannot yet grasp. I imagined the curiosity of a civilization located billions of light years away, deciphering artifacts found on Earth and wondering about the meaning of my hologram, trying to figure out whether it was a billboard ad, a game, a work of art, a religious altar, or all of that, all at once.

For the first time in weeks, I managed to relax a little.

This interstellar intrigue was grandiose.

I had found the epilogue for my mother.

Before going to sleep, I think I heard her whisper in my ear that, even better, in this galaxy far far away, we will join the Eternals.

Together.

Karoline Georges is the author of seven books, including *Sous béton* (a finalist for the 2012 Quebec Booksellers' Prize). In 2012, she received the Artistic Creation Award from the Conseil des arts et des lettres du Québec. Her latest novel, *The Imago Stage*, has won several honours in French, including the Governor General's Literary Award in 2018.

Rhonda Mullins has translated many books into English, including *Suzanne* by Anaïs Barbeau-Lavalette, a finalist for the 2018 Best Translated Book Award and Canada Reads 2019. She won the Governor General's Award for Translation for *Twenty-One Cardinals* by Jocelyne Saucier.

Typeset in Whitman and DIN Condensed

Printed at the Coach House on bpNichol Lane in Toronto, Ontario, on
Zephyr Antique Laid paper, which was manufactured, acid-free, in Saint-
Jérôme, Quebec, from second-growth forests. This book was printed with
vegetable-based ink on a 1973 Heidelberg KORD offset litho press. Its
pages were folded on a Baumfolder, gathered by hand, bound on a Sulby
Auto-Minabinda, and trimmed on a Polar single-knife cutter.

Translated by Rhonda Mullins
Edited by Alana Wilcox
Cover and interior design by Crystal Sikma
Cover image by Karoline Georges
Author photo by Yannick Forest
Translator photo by Owen Egan

Coach House Books
80 bpNichol Lane
Toronto ON M5S 3J4
Canada

416 979 2217
800 367 6360

mail@chbooks.com
www.chbooks.com